*

"A master."

*

"Taibo's is a fresh voice, his approach to the material distinctive."

*

"His novels have injected a freshness into Latin American literature that had been flagging since the boom generation that includes Mario Vargas Llosa [and] Gabriel García Márquez."

*

"The reader discovers a sensibility that could well be the envy of writers who produce psychology and sociology."

*

*

"A wonderful writer. . . . LIFE ITSELF moves at Mach speed from the first page: Staccato chapters, brilliant insights into the writer's life and scathing political satire. . . . Enchanting."

—*Houston Chronicle*

*

"An offbeat crime novel . . . that's partly Mack Sennett goofiness, partly surrealistic, and partly scathing outrage against social injustice."

—*Buffalo News*

*

"Taibo takes a hard-boiled detective story and stretches it into a surreal tapestry. . . . His elliptic use of murder to illuminate the political chaos of his country is wildly funny—and eerie."

—*St. Petersburg Times*

*

NOVELS OF PACO IGNACIO TAIBO II
IN ENGLISH TRANSLATION

An Easy Thing
The Shadow of the Shadow
Some Clouds
No Happy Ending
Four Hands
Leonardo's Bicycle

LIFE ITSELF

PACO IGNACIO TAIBO II

THE MYSTERIOUS PRESS

Published by Warner Books

A Time Warner Company

MYSTERIOUS PRESS EDITION

Copyright © 1990 by Paco Ignacio Taibo II
Translation copyright © 1994 by Paco Ignacio Taibo II and Beth Henson
All rights reserved.

Cover design by Rachel McClain
Cover illustration by José Ortega

The Mysterious Press name and logo are registered trademarks of Warner Books, Inc.

 Mysterious Press books are published by
Warner Books, Inc.
1271 Avenue of the Americas
New York, NY 10020

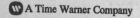 A Time Warner Company

Printed in the United States of America

Originally published in hardcover by The Mysterious Press.
First Printed in Paperback: August, 1995

10 9 8 7 6 5 4 3 2 1

This book is for: Marc Cooper, Los Angeles journalist; Carlos Monsiváis, writer in the Portales; Esther, owner of a bookstore in Zacatecas; Héctor Mercado, attorney; Juan Carlos Canales and Fritz Glockner, from Puebla . . . and for all the minor characters of this story.

And, in the rain, with luck you will see
that in that which gave you life, you fear death.
    Francisco de Quevedo

So, the heroes belong to the books.
    André Malraux

Note: The mining town of Santa Ana in the north-central part of Mexico does not exist, and neither was there a red city government nor a chief of police who wrote detective novels. That story proudly belongs to the terrain of fiction. The majority of its characters exist only in the pages of this book, and even those whose names or distinguishing marks I have taken from life say things that can be attributed only to my imagination. I make this declaration so that nobody thinks, on the other hand, that the country we speak of is not real. It is all too real, and I live with it every day.

Note II: For the non-Mexican reader, the PRI is the official government party that, since the close of the 1920s, has ruled Mexico in a civil dictatorship rife with violence and electoral fraud; members of the PRI are called "priístas." "Cacique" is a term for the political boss of an agrarian zone; originally the word meant "Indian chief." Since the 1920s, Mexican labor unions have operated under heavy government control; in their opposition to these organizations, "red" independents refer to them as "yellow unions."

LIFE ITSELF

1.

Raining in Mexico City

━━━━━━━━━━━━━━━━━━━━━━━━━━━━━━━━━━━━

"If it didn't rain in this city, I would have abandoned it a long time ago," thought José Daniel Fierro, immediately registering and filing the thought. There were ideas that were work, reusable thoughts that made up sentences that were later taken up by the keyboard. The rain-reflection was his, but could be made to serve as that of the old Villista who worked in a hardware store in the middle of the third chapter of the novel he was writing. "If it didn't rain . . ." he wrote at the head of the page, watching the drops of water drum on the double panes near his white table and imagining without hearing the splash, the small plop. He had to get into the sentence a bit of the sound of the wind that pushed the rain against the window and that made a literary image, shaking the solitary laurel of the ridge, making it dance. "If there were no laurel," he could go as well; him, not the old man in chapter three. Every day he wrote about leaving and yet he stayed. He lit a Mapleton from the butt of another. Ana,

seated at his back in a white armchair, looked up from the
book she was reading and stretched out her hand to steal his
cigarette.

"You know what it costs us to smoke?"

José Daniel stroked his big black moustache, watching the
rain.

"Forty-two thousand pesos a month, what do you think of
that? Emphysema is the most expensive disease to acquire in
the world," said Ana, without waiting for a response.

"Once I heard of a syphilis that cost a guy two hundred
thousand pesos."

"That's nothing. A minor matter," said Ana. "Would you
like some coffee?"

"A double cognac."

"Come to think of it, alcoholism is even more expensive,"
she said, walking to the kitchen. The ringing doorbell made
her change direction.

José Daniel Fierro touched his elbow. The rain brought
him a touch of arthritis.

The beginning of a chapter must be convincing. Only a
mediocrity would begin "If it didn't rain in this city . . ."
He tried to keep the conversation in the doorway from breaking his line of thought. He almost had it. He typed, destroying
the foul whiteness of the paper: "A good detective only lives
in cities where it rains like this."

"Daniel, you have visitors," said Ana, almost breathing
the words down his neck.

José Daniel turned and contemplated the three arrivals: a
disheveled young man wearing boots and a jacket and very
thick glasses; a bearded forty year old with a fierce look; a
man of thirty-five, dark, with green eyes, whom he had seen
many times in photographs.

"Come in, sit down," he said to the three, who were
trying not to get mud on the white carpet. They approached,
offering their hands. The writer turned his chair to face them,
offering them the two armchairs; Ana stayed by the door,
vigilant in her role as hostess-proprietor.

"We are from the commission," said the youth with glasses.

"It's raining buckets," said José Daniel, just to say something.

"They called you, didn't they?" asked the man with green eyes.

"You are Benjamín Correa," said the writer, and the youth nodded.

"Macario, leader of Section Twenty-three, and Fritz, director of our radio station," he answered, indicating his two companions.

"No, nobody called me, but there's no problem," said the writer. "What can I do for you? The Festival of Culture in Santa Ana? I already said yes, I would go, and signed the manifesto. It came out today, didn't it?"

"We would like you to sign another little piece of paper," said the leader of the miners.

"A check?"

The three characters laughed.

"No, Compañero Fierro, worse than that," said Fritz Glockner.

José Daniel smiled.

"We want you to be the chief of police of Santa Ana," said the mayor of the radical town. The three laughed again.

José Daniel emitted a doubtful chuckle.

"You want me to write a detective novel about Santa Ana?"

"No. We want you to be chief of police of Santa Ana."

"What in the world!" exclaimed Ana.

"Are you serious?" asked the writer.

"Of course," said Benjamín Correa, lighting up a Delicado without filter. Macario, the miner, assented with a sly smile.

José Daniel Fierro observed them fixedly, trying not to meet his wife's eyes.

"Wait a minute, let me get this straight. You want me to go to Santa Ana and take over the police department? The municipal police?"

The three nodded.

"I think what you're doing is extremely important. Your experience is fundamental in the midst of so much bullshit. As far as it goes. Let's be clear. I sign manifestos, march in demonstrations, write about you where I can if I have something to say, give money, go to Santa Ana to take part in the Festival of Culture; these are things I know how to do, that I can do. Until now, once again . . . To be chief of police is madness. I'm fifty years old . . ."

"Fifty-two," said Ana.

"Fifty-one and my birthday's next month . . ." he answered quickly. "I've never shot a pistol in my life."

"Really?" asked Macario, who found it hard to believe there was anyone in Mexico who had never shot a gun.

"But in *Death in the Afternoon* it tells everything about the .45, the impact, the backfire, the precision, the cleaning . . ." said Fritz Glockner, smiling.

"I got that out of an Italian manual on firearms," the writer apologized. "And moreover, what does it matter? I have no real experience with the police. Only fiction, only literature."

"In *The Head of Pancho Villa* you tell the story of a bank fraud, that's how we knew what was happening in Santa Ana."

"Okay, that's how it happens. Son of a bitch! Do I have to tell you the difference between life and fiction?"

"There is no difference," said the red mayor. "It is only a question of miles. Who does know about the police in Mexico? No one. Only you, the writer. Who has eleven novels published? To be sure, I missed one, the one about the migrant workers . . ."

"*The Line*," said JD. "I have copies around here somewhere . . ."

"Probably what's happening is that we're not explaining it very well," said Fritz. "Look here: in one and a half years they have assassinated two municipal chiefs of police in Santa Ana. The state judicial cops have us by the balls, we need someone good, someone they can't kill without the whole country going up in arms, even the whole world. For example, a writer who just won the Grand Prize for Detective Literature at Grenoble, who gives interviews to the *New York Times*. A left-winger who comes out on Rocha's TV program when he publishes a book. Someone they can't kill, and who has a brain, ideas, an investigative mind, someone who serves the people and freaks out the PRI and the state government. Someone who can make his mark on Santa Ana."

"I understand all that, but you must take something into account. I am a coward. I'm afraid. Every day this country scares me more. If I go on writing and talking it's because I'm even more afraid to keep silent."

"Bravery is no problem, we can handle that part," said the mayor. "We have ten guys who would go into the lion's den, handcuffed, and kick the beasts in the crotch . . . We want someone like you. Just imagine: José Daniel Fierro, chief of police of Santa Ana."

"I can imagine."

"I'll divorce you, do you hear me?" said Ana.

"Whose idea was it?" asked the writer.

"We were looking around, asking people, and Carlos Monsiváis was the one who suggested you."

"Son of a bitch, what an idiot joke."

"Think it over, maestro. You're not only doing us a service in Santa Ana, think of the number of detective novels that you'll get out of it. Our crimes are really far out," said Fritz.

"They've got us by the balls," said the mayor again, and José Daniel realized how he had gotten the job. He put such intensity into his words, he grabbed you by the throat and didn't let go. "They surround us, cut our budget, the bosses hassle us, they cut off the municipal funds, provoke us, surround us with the blackest publicity campaign in the history of Mexico. The elections come up in eight months: if we win, they'll bring in the army, if we lose, they'll tear apart the whole Popular Organization we've created. We need all the help we can get. We need a chief of police . . . What do you say?"

"Does it rain a lot in Santa Ana?"

"Every day," said Macario.

"Never," said Fritz Glockner.

"Say the word," answered the mayor.

"I'll divorce you," said Ana. "I swear I'll divorce you."

2.

Notes for the History of the Radical City Government of
Santa Ana
José Daniel Fierro

▬▬▬▬▬▬▬▬▬▬▬▬▬▬▬▬▬▬▬▬▬▬▬▬▬

I have discovered at least six ways of beginning the history
of the radical city government of Santa Ana, after only one
day in a car on the Pan American Highway heading north
with three singular companions. One of them would be to
tell the story of the struggle of Section 23 of the miners'
union to become independent of the yellow union in the
middle of the 1970s; another would be to follow the threads
of what is called *La Voz del Pueblo*, the weekly paper begun
by Correa seven years ago, which gave birth to the Popular
Organization where the miners united with the students who
had come back home after studying in Guadalajara, Monterrey, or Mexico City; another would be the personal story of
Benjamín Correa, the antlike persistence that led him to know
Santa Ana as no one before him (and when I say *know* I
would have to even include the biblical sense, for the jokes

in the car ran to at least seven "little houses" with wives included, while he remains officially a bachelor); another would have to do with the work that two old communists did here, one a miner named Don Andrés, now retired, and a shopkeeper, who in the end was one of the ones who pushed the experience onto the electoral path. There is a fifth way of approaching the story of the government, which has to do with the people's law office organized by Mercado, which for three years gave legal support to farmers kicked off their land, market vendors, and schoolteachers fired for unjust cause. The sixth way is to follow the trajectory of the genesis of the popular government from the abuses of the PRI bosses to the popular revolt. Just for starters.

My traveling companions in the beat-up Renault suggest the story of the dead as a seventh option: pug-nosed Madera, shot from a hoist when the miners began to organize. The death by a stray bullet of Doña Jerónima, who sold chickens in the marketplace and who fell in the demonstration of the 20th of April. The death of Quintín Ramírez, forty-five-year-old peasant, strung up in the doorway of his hut by the landowners' thugs. The death of seven children in an epidemic at the end of the 1980s. The death of Daniel Contreras, run over by the drunken son of Simpson, manager of the Santa Ana Mining Company. The death of Lisandro Vera, a law student born in Santa Ana and the first chief of police of the popular government, shot as he left the jail. The death of Manuel, a Coca-Cola worker, knifed on the picket line by a scab paid by the company. The death of the schoolteacher Elpidio, the second chief of police of the radical government of Santa Ana, as he pursued a truck loaded with marijuana ten miles outside of town.

That would be another way of telling the story of this city, which until now I only knew by way of photos and which I always imagined as a big ranch full of red flags. Which I am now beginning to see up close: a mixture of cobblestone and asphalt streets, a municipal plaza, and an intricate complex of passions and powers, a bookstore(!), 11 movie theaters,

11 houses of prostitution (known and stable), 3 taxi stands, 117 crimes of passion weekly, 1,654 weddings a year, 231,000 inhabitants, 21 churches, 42 primary schools, 4 middle schools, 1 high school, 3 supermarkets, a movie director, 16 hotels, 28 percent of the country's production of tin, a circus every two months, a radical government that won the elections by 86,000 to 12,000 votes, and a mountain of dust and loose dirt that muddies the mountain air.

3.

Dear Ana/April 13

Dear Ana/April 13
   Well, so here I am, looking out over the town from my window in the Hotel Florida (I pushed a bureau over to the window and set up my office; the typewriter is up very high, I hope I don't hurt my back since the chair is very low). I hope you are not in a rush to accuse me of abandonment, but if I were to sit down and talk it over with you, I would never leave home. Send me a package by Frontier Bus Lines, a bunch of black ribbons for the Olivetti portable, the cotton ones they sell at the shop on the corner, as well as the original, which is in a red briefcase with a lock, and a pile of novels by J. P. Machette that I left on my side of the bed, there's maybe seven of them, you'll find them immediately. And if it's not too much trouble, send me the bottle of gringo aspirins, the ones with the sealed cap, and the blue turtleneck sweater.

Don't ask me what I'm doing in Santa Ana, I still don't know, and if I tried to explain it to you now it would be pure rhetoric. Forgive me, one more time in so many years.

Kisses. JD

4.

Hotel Florida

It was dawn and the light from the east filtered slowly down the main street of Santa Ana, illuminating the white houses at three hundred yards and licking the nearest walls.

From his room on the fourth floor of the Hotel Florida José Daniel Fierro thought that he would never be able to reveal the quality of that light; that he could be chief of police of Santa Ana, because life is sufficiently strange and creates roads, waterfalls, and bends in the roads, but that he would never be able to tell anyone just how that soft light came advancing toward him, entering into his room.

Because chiefs of police improvise, but the narrators of dawn are the product of years of words.

His eyes were irritated by sleeplessness, but the window drew him like brown and sticky flypaper, the kind that no longer exists, which he remembered from childhood vacations in Veracruz.

From the window of his hotel room he could see ten or

twelve streets, even the main avenue, which curved away toward the north and hid itself behind a four-story building with a movie theater on the first floor. A solitary street, with its lights still on, useless in the precipitant approach of dawn.

José Daniel searched in his travel bag for a flask and wet his lips with warm cognac. The whole town was covered with graffiti: sidewalks, fences, light poles, columns, even some low rooftops, house fronts, walls, trees. All painted over many times and by many hands, in many styles; differing hands piling up slogans and signs, advice and insult, calls to conscience, logos of the Popular Organization, calls to the future, memories of the past, cryptic half-written warnings whose final rushing letters fell to the ground.

The walls told the story of the last two years in Santa Ana, inviting one to think of the heat of a bonfire, of malevolence, of verbal warfare. Who said that revolutions advance on a highway of words?

José Daniel Fierro winked an eye at the principal street of Santa Ana and promised himself to buy a notebook and write down what the walls were saying, even to take a few photos.

"Chief of Police, sir, I want you to meet the assistant chief of police," said the voice of Benjamín Correa at his back.

José Daniel turned around.

"Barrientos, alias—more than alias, official name—Blind Man."

A short man of square shoulders and body, with eyeglasses of fifteen diopters on each side, moustache and eyebrows that met in the middle, smiled at him, almost thrusting his teeth out of his mouth.

"Pleased to meet you."

"The pleasure is mine, sir," said the short man, fluttering his eyes behind the heavy lenses. "I have already read six of your novels. The one I liked best is the one about Pancho Villa."

"Thanks a lot, man," said José Daniel, ceremoniously offering his hand.

"They call him Blind Man because he can shoot the balls

off a fly with a .45 at forty yards. Not because he's near-sighted," declared the mayor.

"That's good to know."

"The official inauguration will be tomorrow morning, but Blind Man tells me that while we were gone there was an assassination, so I thought . . ."

José Daniel looked at the dawn from the corner of his eye, as if to memorize it, gave another pull on his flask of cognac and smiled timidly.

"Let's go."

She was a campesina of thirty, with her hands firmly clasped, her eyes irritated by tears that were no longer there, wearing a blue blouse printed with flower garlands.

"They tell me you killed your husband, señora, why did you do that?"

The woman looked at her hands, which were dried up by years of work.

"With a machete? You gave him six blows with a machete while he was sleeping? How did this happen, señora?"

She was seated on a cot in the cell, barely lit by the sixty-watt bulb that hung from a wire.

"Her name is Margarita," said Blind Man.

"Let's see, Doña Margarita, why did you kill him? or are you going to say that you didn't kill him? Because we found you with the machete in your hand, next to the dead man, just you and him in the room, and him in bed . . . Tell me why."

The woman lifted her head, looked at José Daniel for a moment, and then looked at the little window where the light was beginning to come in.

"Who is this gentleman?" she asked Blind Man without looking at him.

"He is the chief of police, señora."

"Did we appoint him ourselves?"

"He was appointed by Benjamín. He's very knowledge-able."

"Do they feed us in here?"

"Three times a day, señora, not like before."

"And why does he want to know?"

"To be sure it was you, so we don't make a mistake, and so justice is done," said José Daniel.

"Justice has been done," said the woman and looked at him from the corner of her eye.

"What justice? To kill a man is justice?"

The woman did not answer.

Blind Man took José Daniel by the arm and led him to the door of the cell. They walked out toward the street.

"You don't lock the cell?"

"They lock the door to the passage that leads to the cells, Mateo will lock it now. We have no prisoners today, they left for the weekend."

"Take me to the crime site, Barrientos."

"Sir, call me Blind Man. If you don't I'll feel weird."

"We are all blind, that's what the lady would say."

"That's what she said, but the blows were well placed."

"Why?"

"Only she and God know," said Blind Man.

"According to my enormous knowledge of criminal themes, this is known by herself, God, and the neighbors . . . page one hundred sixty-three of *Dead without Memory*."

"I didn't read that one," said Blind Man.

"You didn't miss much," said José Daniel, lighting a Mapleton and offering one to his companion, who tore off the filter before lighting it. "Do we have a patrol car?"

"Two motorcycles, two bicycles, and a Volkswagen with a grille between the seats, but it's out patrolling the town. You'll see . . . We'll walk, it's toward the La Gracia neighborhood."

José Daniel let himself be guided by the rapid pace of Blind Man, closing his eyes even more against the sunlight. They walked down alleyways and left the asphalt to start on dirt roads and cobblestones; they soon began to run into milkmen, miners in khaki overalls, women carrying fruit and vegetables to market. It was cold.

"You're going to like it here," said Blind Man. "Something happens all the time."

José Daniel agreed.

5.

Notes for the History of the Radical City Government of
Santa Ana
José Daniel Fierro

▲▲▲▲▲▲▲▲▲▲▲▲▲▲▲▲▲▲▲▲▲▲▲▲▲▲▲▲▲▲▲▲

Benjamín Correa is thirty-two years old, a medical doctor,
graduate of the National University of Mexico (UNAM), born
in Santa Ana. This is a recording that I made of him while
we came here. To be overly precise, it was on the long
straightaway between San Luis and Matehuala, where you
talk for a long time, pouring your heart out, because the
highway without trees or lights makes you cough up everything you've got inside. The punctuation is mine.

Correa: . . . forgive me, writer. You could be moved by
other things: by prestige, a cold conscience, responsibility,
hatred, whatever; me, by guilt. Santa Ana and I are married
by fucking guilt. Better yet, by guilts: better to speak of many
guilts. In 1976 I went to Mexico City to begin my courses,
and they said to me, "Stay for the demonstration, it's going
to be good," and I took to the road and left. I already knew

enough medicine to cure the wounded, and on the next day there were thirty people wounded by gunfire, by sticks, by dog bites, by machete, and the asshole was in his classroom studying X rays of the chests of old Swiss gentlemen, because this is what the professor had to show, to see if they had tuberculosis in 1950 and how. And here they died alone. My cousin Evelia with two bullets in her belly . . . There's no mystery. Just guilt. And that's just one, there are many more. I have a list, this long!, of all the times I was quiet, of all the times I ran, of all the times I gave in . . . Now I sleep well, and if they kill me, I'll sleep even better. If everyone did what they had to, we'd be better off. That's the key to the game of the Popular Organization. Ask the people to each do what they have to do, not what would be better, not what would be more convenient, nor more beneficial, nor more revolutionary. Just simply what they have to do.

JDF: It sounds good. It's the best political theory I've heard in the last few years.

Benjamín Correa: It sounds like shit. If we lose, they'll send the town back to the nineteenth century.

JDF: The nineteenth century was a son of a bitch, Juarista liberalism and all that.

Benjamín Correa: To the nineteenth century of Santa Ana.

Fritz: You're very apocalyptic, one would have to . . .

Macario: They're going to cut off our balls.

Benjamín Correa: I hope they leave me something, because we're all going to be just delighted with our dicks made into mincemeat.

Macario: Don't scare the chief of police, assholes . . . Do you like frijoles charros? Here in Santa Ana they're bitching.

JDF: A while ago . . .

Benjamín Correa: Pure guilt, do you understand?

6.

The Baseball Cap

"That shirt fits you perfectly, chief," said Blind Man.

The city provided the police uniform: brown shirt and trousers, a sheep-lined jacket for cold, Stetson hat or baseball cap. José Daniel chose the baseball cap with the inscription SANTA ANA WILL WIN above the visor. A little brunette rummaged a long time to find pants in his size in the cooperative store; "long and with a bit of belly" according to Blind Man.

They left the store, full of people at eight in the morning. José Daniel smiled, he felt "uniformed" and moreover had found two of his novels with yesteryear's prices in the shop.

"Do I get a sheriff's badge?" he asked his second-in-command.

"The truth is, I never asked. They do give ID."

"Without a badge, I feel half out of uniform," said José Daniel, stopping at a toy stand. He picked through the buttons: there were Snoopys, ALL YOU NEED IS LOVE, Che Guevara,

the Sandinista Front, Rafael and Rocío Durcal. He chose one
that showed Spiderman in a posture of challenge.

"Do you want one?"

"I don't think so," said Blind Man.

José Daniel pinned it on his new shirt.

"Okay now. One madness more or less . . . Hell, I feel
thirty years old."

"Me too."

"How old are you?"

"Shit, I'm twenty-eight."

They walked around the downtown area. Low buildings
that opened to shared central patios, grocery shops. Everything painted. Everything, not one inch of free space. Beer
advertisements everywhere. Blind Man led him to an enormous public building. José Daniel began to get his bearings:
City Hall here, the hotel, the jail . . .

He climbed a high stairway with a half-finished mural that
showed the devil, Reagan, and two men in sombreros playing
cards.

"Who are they?"

"The old boss and his brother, the Barrios. The PRI bosses
in Santa Ana. You had to remind me of their faces. Those two
screw us over more than Reagan and the devil put together."

The stairs led to a balustrade around a central patio with
a colonial fountain. The offices, with their doors of white
wood in doorways carved of quarrystone, bore enormous
letters: COORDINATOR OF CULTURE, MEDICAL DISPENSARY,
RADIO SANTA ANA, CHIEF OF POLICE.

"This whole side of the building is ours. This and the jail
are ours. The mayor and the sombrero cooperative occupy
the left wing."

In the doorway of Radio Santa Ana, Fritz was arguing with
a delegation of middle school students who were demanding
that he let them broadcast a soap opera about *Chucho the
Broken*, directed by the professor of dramatic arts. Fritz
waved and pointed to José Daniel's new cap.

Blind Man opened the door of the police office, removing
an enormous iron padlock.

"Half of the personnel are here, you'll see them soon. The
others are in the offices down the side. This office is just for
you."

It was a room worthy of Philip Marlowe. A wooden desk
made in the 1950s, venetian blinds that let in slits of light,
a coat rack for hanging nonexistent trench coats and hats,
two gray metal file cabinets with signs of having been
forced with a crowbar, a chair on wheels, and a reclining
chair with slats on the back. A new coffee maker, strangely
out of place.

Blind Man met José Daniel's eyes.

"The coffee maker belongs to Elpidio. Okay, belongs to
his widow. That was the only thing he brought. Nothing
else."

José Daniel walked slowly to his chair, let himself fall,
and put his feet on the desk. He pushed back the visor of his
cap and half closed his eyes to dream other dreams.

"Elpidio's pistol is in the drawer. Since you don't know
shit about it, anything will do, although I recommend a shotgun, because it shoots wholesale and hits anything at ten
yards."

"How serious are things around here?" asked José Daniel,
stretching to turn on the coffee maker, "because I feel like
I'm in the movies, and in the movies . . . No, wait, in a
novel, and as Malraux said, heroes are from literature."

"What do you mean, serious?" asked Blind Man, letting
himself fall on a three-legged stool in front of the desk.
"Serious as in do people kill? Yes, they kill, and to tell you
the truth, I don't like it. I don't like it when they kill in cold
blood. I don't like it when they kill and then celebrate. I
don't like it when they let fear loose in the streets. This was
the land of the bosses, sir, a company town; here they beat
you up for breathing, and even more for smiling. There's a
lot of bastards still running around loose . . . A lot of fucking

bastards running around loose. And they don't like what we're doing.''

"And what are we doing?" said José Daniel, staring at the assistant chief of his yet-unseen police force of his still half-guessed-at city.

"Popular power, my good man. What kind of a fucking question is that, excuse me? Do you think you could be chief of police of a PRI town?"

"Of no town, more likely . . . What did you do before, Blind Man? Before you were a cop?"

"Secretary of the Interior of the taxi drivers' union."

"Why did you change jobs?"

"There are things that have to be done. Hasn't that ever happened to you?"

"I don't really know what happened to me. Do you know what it's like to be fifty years old?"

"Not yet, but I'm getting there . . . Although I'm not rushing.''

"It's like knowing that everything's over, bullshit like that . . . I have gray in my moustache, you know that?"

"Blind Man, run, Blind Man, get a move on!" cried a voice that materialized into a hairy and charmless personage who ran into the office red-faced.

"Say hello to the chief, Greñas."

"Chief," said Greñas, saluting. "I report an emergency. They say that the girls are calling for help from the bathroom of El Refugio. A kidnapping, that is. I have the car."

"Did you see them?"

"I was told."

"Let's go, said another blind man," said José Daniel, getting up and feeling the cramp in his knee.

The patrol car was a dented Volkswagen, scarred with rust, painted red and black in two horizontal stripes. Greñas took the wheel, Blind Man gave José Daniel the back seat to shrink into.

"My legs don't fit."

"We should have taken the bike."

"Should I turn on the siren?" asked Greñas.

"No way."

Raising dust, the car ran a dozen blocks and stopped by some department stores on the main street. The trio entered the store, as if pushed by a childish hand to some promising place. They crossed the women's clothing department and were advancing through fabrics when they were stopped.

"Where are you going, Blind Man?" asked a man in a suit, standing in their way and blocking the back part of the counters.

"Are you speaking to the assistant police chief of Santa Ana?" asked José Daniel in full drag, changing from Bogart into Clint Eastwood and pointing a finger at the suited man's belly. "You are obstructing a police inquiry."

"My ass," said the man, slapping off the writer's accusatory finger.

"We know you have some girls shut up in the bathrooms," said Blind Man with his .45 in hand.

"In the women's john. They shut themselves in."

Fifty shoppers were closing in.

Greñas advanced toward the passage behind the counters. They passed the perfume section and the electrical appliances. Far off they saw people running. José Daniel followed the hurried steps of his aides.

Two men were standing by the women's john. The door was surrounded by empty boxes, cardboard tubes that had served as towel holders, and great pieces of granulated polyethylene used to pack stoves and refrigerators; they gave the end of the passage the air of the backstage of a theater.

"Look here, the big honcho of the CTM*, neither more nor less," said Blind Man, pointing to a fat man in a blue shirt standing in front of the door.

"Are you in line for the women's bathroom, sir?" asked José Daniel, doing a Lew Archer with a light touch of Woody Allen.

---

*Federation of Mexican Workers, a yellow union.

Blind Man, more expeditious, motioned for them to move away with the barrel of his revolver.

"Are they here?" cried Greñas.

"Let us out . . . We're not going to sign," came a chorus from behind the door.

Greñas tried the knob. Locked.

"Get back," he yelled, and knocked down the flimsy door with a roundhouse kick.

The onlookers, including the owner of the department store, were milling about in the aisles. José Daniel lit his last Mapleton and threw the empty package on the floor.

Four women came through the door, tripping over themselves and pushing the bystanders.

"They locked us up to make us sign with the CTM," said one to Blind Man. "They hit me."

"They said we would stay here without food until we signed," said a young cross-eyed woman, smiling. The bystanders returned her smile.

"Who locked you up, ladies?" asked José Daniel.

"Domínguez, the owner."

"Him, Domínguez, and the yellow leader of the CTM, Martín Guerra, that revolting fathead."

"None of that, now," threatened the fathead.

"To jail with the two of them, Blind Man," said José Daniel. "Accused of kidnapping. We'll indict them right now."

The bystanders raised a timid applause.

Blind Man moved the barrel of his gun alternately between the owner and the union honcho. In a low voice he asked the new police chief, "Are you sure?"

"Lock them up and we'll see," replied José Daniel Fierro, who then, very nicely, in full Robert Mitchum, offered his arm to the young cross-eyed woman.

7.

Dear Ana/April 14

Dear Ana/April 14
For now, more vaudeville than tragedy, although there's something in the air that tugs at the corners of the eyes and sometimes you walk with a wrinkled brow. A little while ago I took official possession of the role of chief of police of Santa Ana. Attended by friends from the Popular Organization, bystanders, and journalists from Mexico City, Monterrey, and Torreón. Who runs the public relations department of the radical town? They do a wonderful job. The idea that Benjamín and the town leaders drill into me, that the town must call on all possible help, they keep very firmly in mind.

Do I take myself as a joke or do I take myself seriously? I'm laughing at myself a little bit, but Benjamín's speech at my inauguration made my hands sweat. For a few minutes I felt part of a project that fights for survival in a country defeated by so much cynicism, shamelessness, official lies, and barbarity running around loose. That country we know in Mexico City that appears to have no end in sight, that tells us day after day that we're among the defeated, that every dream is impossible except for the nightmare that is installed here among us.

So I opt for the middle road. I regard myself as a joke, but I take very seriously the experiment of the radical city government of Santa Ana.

And by the way, it's true, there's material here for a dozen novels, although I will never be able to write them.

The local radio station is in the office next to me. You would love it. They are the most extraterrestrial people I have met in Santa Ana. Fritz, the coordinator of production, is mounting speakers on the telephone poles. He produces agricultural programs, epic radio novels, radical commercials, at the same time avoiding a system of interference put out from a neighboring peak by the state government to prevent diffusion of the signal. Juan Carlos Canales, incredibly tall and thin, who acts as announcer, master of ceremonies, and funder of the project, told me two things he's working on this week. One, a live program on the prostitutes of Santa Ana (in which they denounce the owners of the brothels and organize), and a radio novel based on the Bible with a Priísta as Lucifer.

My joints ache. I suppose because the town is so dry. Now it's beginning to get cold, send me the aspirins.

I love you from afar. JDF

8.

Rum during Office Hours

―――――――――――――

"Sit down, Chief of Police."

"I sit, Mayor."

"Would you like a rum?"

"I don't drink during working hours."

"I beg your pardon?"

"No, man, I'm putting you on. It's just that all of a sudden I'm getting to say things I've never had the chance to say before. This town is sending my head to a piece of Hollywood that I had tucked away in a corner of my brain."

"It sounded like bullshit to me, because except for the time when I'm sleeping, when I can't drink, every other hour in Santa Ana is a working hour; and without any liquor at all we'd be worse off than we are now."

"I'm seeing a rum on table two, Mayor."

Benjamín Correa took the rum from God knows where under his desk, in a paper cup but with ice and all, and put it in front of José Daniel Fierro. Behind his back was the red and black flag with the logo of the Popular Organization, but missing were the photos of radicals—there was just one displayed. José Daniel made an effort. That photo in particular he had never seen before, but remembered others of the same man from a chain of prisoners: Librado Rivera.

"You have an anarchist on your wall?"

"I keep him because when I despair I read his biography. No one understood better than he did that the revolution in Mexico will be a case of stubbornness."

José Daniel Fierro sipped his rum, letting it heat up his throat. If he continued his Hollywood repertoire, he could choose between Bogart and Peter Lorre: cynical or apparently stupid. He chose Fred Astaire. He stood up and danced a few steps of tap, then smiled.

"In the 1950s I attended an academy of dance. We danced to a piece by Tommy Dorsey till we were exhausted, it must have been the only record they had. What were you doing then?"

"I was a child in the 1950s, Chief Fierro . . . Wasn't Chief Fierro one of the mice in the Mickey Mouse comic books?"

"Damned if I know . . . and so? How'm I doing?"

"Fifty percent."

"I'm all ears."

"Here everything is politics, and arresting the owner of one of the big department stores and the head honcho of the CTM is political. And you have to be very careful with this, because if we push them too hard, they will bring in the army and the experiment will be over. That is the fifty percent bad; before getting into things like that, you have to talk it over with us. This is what I've learned in the last two years."

"And the fifty percent good?"

"That with pressure, we'll force them to let the girls remain in the democratic union instead of making them go with the yellows."

"Will there be a trial?"

"How can there not be, if all the judges are with them?"

"I take note, Brother Mayor," said José Daniel Fierro, slapping his baseball cap against his thighs and standing up.

"Where did you get the Spiderman button?"

"I bought it here. Why?"

"Get me one, would you?"

9.

Dispatches Cast on the Wind

He guided his reading with one finger. The breeze that crossed between the two windows moved the pages and he had to hold them with his left hand. Blind Man walked from one side of the room to the other, stopping to watch him every three steps, to be sure he wasn't losing pages, that no paragraphs jumped out, and no letters were eaten.

"Two big ones, three small ones," said José Daniel with his finger on the final comma of the final sentence of the last dispatch.

"Two big ones, three little ones," repeated Blind Man and re-counted with his fingers, so that not a detail was lost between hand and memory.

"That is what we have pending."

"Plus what happens every day," remembered Blind Man.

José Daniel agreed. Not only the breeze entered the windows, but also a number of songs of the Spanish Civil War. He had heard nearly all of them in the home of his sister who was married to the son of exiles. He himself was a foreigner. In only two days he was an absolute and total stranger. It was not bad. Not bad at all. Not at all bad.

"So, when do I get my pistol?"

"I already thought about it, and it seems to me we should give you Lacho Vázquez's shotgun; with that you could shoot a plow at five yards. Breech loading, six shots, cheap ammunition. The city can afford it and you won't kill anyone by accident."

"Blind Man, you don't have much confidence in me."

"You're a champ at reading dispatches, Señor Chief of Police. You read them three times faster than me."

"Which should we start with?"

"Up to you . . . Are we speaking in tú or usted?"

"As the wind blows."

"Then why don't we start with one of the small ones. The shooting at the tavern on Calle Cuatro a week ago."

"I need a chalkboard," said José Daniel.

"What are you going to give classes in?"

"In the detective novel, my esteemed assistant, and I want that agent who signs himself Luix Lómax."

"Popochas."

"Yes, indeed."

"I'll be right back," said Blind Man, and left to do his assignments. José Daniel lit another cigarette and took his flask from his back pocket. He had gone from Mapletons to Delicados with filter, and from Spanish brandy to cane alcohol. Wasn't this an obvious sign of proletarianization? That morning he had slipped out of bed at the Hotel Florida with the firm intention of comparing Santa Ana with other cities. He had proposed to demonstrate that Santa Ana was better than Reims and Houston, than Seville and Maracaibo. He had only to find the right arguments. Write them, put them down on paper and it would be true. However, the blank paper had won the battle. Son of a whore, cane alcohol was worse than the combustible oxygen gas the taxis used in Madrid. The blank paper won the battle. Right now he had to make history instead of writing it. What history? This, two guys wounded in a tavern? Santa Ana was better than Rome because here the couples walked hand in hand through the square full of shame and made love an act of innocence. On a piece of paper he wrote a name, "Barrio." Underneath he wrote, "Seville, birds, bread." He poured out another shot of alcohol. He could lay aside the toothbrush forgotten in Mexico City. The local cane alcohol did the job very well.

"Ready, chief," said Blind Man, entering the office with a borrowed chalkboard.

"And Popochas?"

"On his way; I had him called over the radio. Since the whole town is full of loudspeakers, we'll have him here in no time."

"Let's see, Blind Man, let's reconstruct," said José Daniel professorially. "We have a tavern with seven people, right? Let's sit them down."

"Where?" asked Blind Man.

"On the chalkboard. Then we're going to ask ourselves who they are. Then we're going to find out why five of them don't want to say who shot at the two who were wounded, then we're going to ask ourselves why the two wounded don't want to say who shot them, then we're going to ask ourselves whose gun was on the floor, what was the trajectory of the bullets . . . We're going to ask ourselves what they were eating, who they were, what the fuck they wanted from life, and how they were dressed."

"All that on a chalkboard?"

"That's what it's good for, to erase when it's full and to start over again. What, you never do paraffin tests here?"

"Why should we when they would all come out positive?"

"Improve your sense of humor, Assistant Barrientos."

"You'll see . . . As Canales—a poet as well as an announcer—says, everything is contagious, even love."

10.

Notes for the History of the Radical City Government of Santa Ana
José Daniel Fierro

▲▲▲▲▲▲▲▲▲▲▲▲▲▲▲▲▲▲▲▲▲▲▲▲▲▲

There are two dates that are regularly cited in conversations with the Popular Organization, the popular forces of Santa Ana: the demonstration of April 20 and the meeting of December 24. Curiously, I do not recall the date of the electoral victory (I believe it fell in August) among the material gleaned from conversations turning around in my head. It would appear, and here one is once again interpreting instead of narrating, as if the victory was the result of the Demonstration—with a capital D, although I must have been told of three others that have their own particular names and glory. The demonstration when Lacho climbed up City Hall by the portals like an African ape or the demonstration with gunfire in 1973 or the demonstration that lasted two days. But the Demonstration was that of April 20, and, in the parlance of radical Santa Ana, December 24 has nothing to do with Santa

Claus or the birth of Christ Jesus but instead has to do with the Meeting.

I tell you because collective memory is perhaps the best political evaluator, the best revealer of realities, the best index of importance. I tell you what they tell me. I don't even know which came first, the meeting of December 24 or the demonstration of April 20. I would guess that logically the meeting preceded the demonstration by a few months and that by then the Popular Organization already existed.

The characters are alike and different. The Meeting, in the talk of the PO and the popular militants, made equal stars of Benjamín, the lawyer Mercado, old Güicho, and the dead ex-chief of police and teachers' leader, Elpidio. It also has its celebrated phrase, "If they don't stop talking bullshit, I'll shoot myself to show an example," uttered by Don Güicho. And its amulets: Don Güicho's pistol, the bloody shirt of Quintín Ramírez, on which all or nothing is sworn, and the Panama hat my assistant Barrientos wore that day that everyone remembers (I must remember to ask him what the hell happened to that hat).

The Demonstration is more properly common property. Everyone has his six or seven personal favorites: Benjamín Correa, of course, Elpidio, who was at his side, the narrator himself, a cousin of his who was passing through, Lacho, and Doña Caro and Doña Jerónima, now dead. It has its slogan: "Let them kill us all, dead we are real motherfuckers," coined by Benjamín to stop people from running away when the shooting started. And it has its own place, engraved forever in memory by blood and stone: the corner of the square, entering from Benito Juárez, where the flower cart and the taco stand stood.

Now a few years have passed, a very few years, and there is a communal middle school, full of teenagers in green uniforms, whom I see every day at dawn walking down the highway into town, and the school is named April 20. The kids, happy kids, smile like an interminable toothpaste ad and know why the school is named that way. Some of them

marched in the demonstration, some of them picked up the
wounded. They have their own version of what happened.
They have their own hierarchy of memories. The smallest
speak of the machine gun at the palace, with two feet, no
three, supported on the balustrade. The big ones speak of the
blood that flowed down Benjamín's white shirtfront, and how
everyone believed he was dead, and that no, it turned out the
blood was not his, it belonged to other people.

Yesterday I asked Benjamín whose blood it was. And he
instantly replied, "Everyone's."

When I write these notes, I have to keep that bloody shirt
in mind, so I'm not fooled by the peaceful cobblestone streets,
the occasional car that passes in front of the Hotel Florida,
and the treacherous light, the marvelous dawn in Santa Ana.

11.

Dear Ana/April 15

━━━━━━━━━━━━━━━━━━━━━━━━━━━━━━━━━━━━

Dear Ana/April 15
  Domestic tales:
  I have gone to Delicados with filter. First, I smoked Mapletons because you stole them from me, and I liked the way the house smelled. It turns out I don't like them so much now that no one is smoking at my side. Second, they are hard to come by in Santa Ana. Third, everyone I offer them to looks at me strangely. Populism has its eccentricities.
  I have a voracious appetite. I eat whatever they give me in emormous quantities.
  I have a baseball cap (I'm enclosing a photo you can send to my nephew Marcial). You see me not only with the cap on but in full small-town sheriff drag. Without comment. The local correspondent of *unomásuno* took it, so I suppose it will come out in the paper. Did anyone call you with the

news? Tell the editors not to worry, the novel will be ready by the middle of May, as we had agreed.

I'm cold and sleepy. I don't want to read this note, I'll find out I'm illiterate and infantile. I'm happy.

Yes I love you: JD

12.

There's Nothing like a Lawyer

"**W**hoever is free from madness, let him cast the first stone," said José Daniel Fierro to himself while he thought how ridiculous it was to sleep switching his pajama tops and bottoms on alternate days. Later he advanced to further reflections and made a list of his own idiosyncracies while he rubbed his eyes furiously, trying to open them to the light:

a) Making orange juice by hand, even when he had an electric juicer in the house. Idiocy that he defended against wind and tide, to the extent of cutting the cord of the electric juicer when Ana suggested repairing it, since he concealed his madness by saying it was broken.

b) Opening his sandwiches to eat the two halves separately, for which all sandwich makers have hated him for the past forty-five years of his life, seeing him as a destroyer of the art of the sandwich, a violator of tradition, and a dirty son of a bitch who should roast in hell.

c) Urinating sitting down. A feminine habit, dangerous in case of discovery, which originated a thousand years ago with the pleasure of reading shut up in the bathroom, isolated, sequestered behind a locked door and secure from disturbances from the outside.

d) Picking the wax from his ears with a match and then setting it on fire, although it almost never caught, but limited itself to an acrid and foolish smell.

He stopped his list, which could go on indefinitely, and dressed only in a pajama top walked to the window of his room, ready as ever to let Santa Ana enter his eyes before he accepted it in his mind. The city was there.

The knock on the door did not surprise him. He was waiting. Santa Ana was like that. First it entered the eyes, tamely, then it knocked at the door. He tried to put on his pajama bottoms while preparing to say, "Come in," and almost made it. His "Come in" was uttered while he caught his right foot and fell, trying to hold himself up on the gilded metal post at the foot of the bed. He did not succeed. The attorney Héctor Mercado found the sheriff of Santa Ana rubbing his knee with his balls in the air.

"Are you hurt?"

"Shit in a box," he said, employing a curse he had learned twenty years ago in Salamanca, when he had lived there on scholarship studying the literature of Spain's Golden Age.

Mercado turned his head away to laugh.

"Laugh all you like, there's nothing sillier than someone who falls to fucking pieces at seven in the morning."

Mercado walked to the bed and sat on it, after leaving his briefcase, which was always with him, by the washstand. He was younger than JD, some ten years younger; he would be approaching or just past forty years old, with juvenile whiskers and dusty hair, a bit stiff, a characteristic common to Santa Ana, upon which JD had speculated and noted on a piece of paper, "the water? loose dirt all over the city?" José Daniel could not avoid raising his hand to his own hair as he pulled the string on his pajamas to pull them up. His hair was rough. He would spend half his salary on lemon shampoo, or apple. The Señor Clairol he carried inside attacked him again.

"And what brings you here, Mercado?"

"The mayor sent me to have a brief word with you about the elephant traps of legality to cover your ass a bit."

"Are there many?"

"No, for me it's easy. I will explain to you the jurisdiction in which you should remain. If you want to go further, consult us and we will all decide together if we all go, if you go alone, or if you stay quiet. It is more or less simple. We're all here to serve the people, that's rule number one. How to serve the people, that's open to interpretation. The ones who're out to fuck the people over interpret it the opposite way. The law is written on paper. You follow it to serve the people, you abandon it to go on serving. The only real law is moral . . . Things like that."

"It sounds like a complicated business to me."

"Complicated it is. Get dressed and we'll have a breakfast for big people and I'll tell you about it."

JD looked in the mirror. What he saw did not bother him too much. He could live inside the guy he saw in the mirror. He had gray hairs in his moustache. They were his.

Half an hour later, with plates of eggs before them, Mercado said: "The municipal police are preventative, their work is limited to making arrests in flagrante or by denunciation. In other words, it is the first recourse of law. Simpler cases go to the justice of the peace, who can in turn pass judgment on minor or administrative infractions. All the bigger cases go to the state, where the Public Ministry orders investigations, and remands them to the state judiciary and not the local municipal police. They take charge of common crimes, robbery, murder, rape. Their prisoners go to the state penitentiary. In cases of drug trafficking, treason to the country, and contraband, the Federal Public Ministry takes charge and the feds intervene, under charge of the attorney general of the republic. The municipal police can testify in serious cases and help in investigations, that is to say, they can lend a hand.''

"And where does all this leave us?"

Mercado took his time in chewing an enormous mouthful of eggs and tortilla.

"It leaves us in the middle . . . We have no federal agents here, and when we do they're up to no good. We have a judicial detachment, led by Durán Rocha, a very well connected gangster. You'll see for yourself. We have an agent of the state Public Ministry, who in turn has a pair of agents under him whom you'll meet soon. What that means for now is that all major investigations will be impeded and that when you detain a murderer in flagrante, the state will let him go after a rigged trial in the capital, and so on.''

"And so what do I do?"

"The best you can, my friend. I remind you of the cardinal rule: when it's a big deal, consult us and we'll see how to make it smaller.''

JD gazed at the lawyer with dirty hair. Nothing was clear.

13.

Notes for the History of the Radical City Government of
Santa Ana
José Daniel Fierro

Santa Ana has a hit parade of sons of bitches. They have
certain similarities to the national hit parade. If you study
them, you find small oscillations, minor variations like raising
the son-in-law to number seven instead of leaving him at the
fifteen that he averages. Nevertheless, in the judgment of
Benjamín Correa, the hit parade is not exact. I always thought
the advantage and disadvantage of the class struggle (as in
wrestling) is knowing the enemy, the conversion of symbols
into names, the personification of constant capital and the
agricultural bourgeoisie as Jack and Jill. Correa maintains
that no, Santa Ana has its own lights and shadows, its own
endowment of classist zebras, full of white or black lines as
you wish to see them. That is his theory and he got it somewhere, and I don't doubt his virtue as an observer. However,
in view of the fact that his information stays at the enigmatic

level of maintaining doubts, I keep in mind the results of the survey I've made in the last few days:

Indisputable number one in the hit parade: Melchor Barrio, boss of the PRI, brother of the phantasmal agrarian cacique, toothless and with bad breath; in delincuential material (maybe it's not said like that but the word enchants me), violator of minors of age.

Number two and hard on the heels of the one before and not only figuratively, Sabás, just like that, Don Sabás if you're being polite. Homeowner, brother-in-law of the former, and yet they don't get along and have bad blood between them. They say that Melchor killed a son of Sabás's years ago in a fight over land. Sabás's crimes are not clear, he appears to be mixed up in everything and nothing. He is whispered to be involved in marijuana traffic with the ranches north of Santa Ana. Very friendly with the chief of the judicial police, one Durán Rocha, number four on the list despite only six months in town.

Number three, all agree, and numbers one and two on certain anonymous lists, Manuel Reyna, Blackie. A hired gun who runs the shock troops of the PRI in Santa Ana. Responds directly to the will of the state capital, doesn't treat with the local powers. Everyone says it was he who fired on the April 20 demonstration with a machine gun from the church tower. Someone told me that before being a gunman he sold agricultural equipment. They call him Blackie because he's an albino. Good to know that. Better to notice him from afar. Someone told me that he doesn't sleep in Santa Ana, that he keeps his cot in González Ortega, a small town that is the head of the neighboring municipality, about nineteen miles northeast of Santa Ana.

A tie for number five between the bosses of the CTM and the CROC,* half a dozen of one and half a dozen of the other. They even look alike. The difference might be that

*Revolutionary Confederation of Workers and Peasants, another yellow union.

Martín Guerra, as well as being a union honcho (now all he's got is a pair of unions maintained by force by the bosses), is the owner of three butcher shops that the PO has been boycotting in response to a call put out by Radio Santa Ana, which has made him purple with rage.

Place number seven is collective, divided between the foremen of the mine and the gringo director, who is not out and about town these days because he is having his balls operated on in Houston, as I've been told by my agent Lómax, who is involved with his maid.

In eighth place, a lawyer, mentioned little but always by those who are well informed, Querejeta, from Mexico City, who wears dark glasses and sleeps in the hotel across the street from mine, as much a stranger here as me, a bird of misfortune who carries disgrace in his luggage.

The list goes on to contain some two hundred and seven more sons of bitches.

14.

Nothing like a Few Shots Before Dinner

He remembered a quote from Ross Macdonald that appropriately explained what happened in the middle of dinner. The one that went: "He was less a man of action than a man of interrogation, a conscience from which the significance of other lives emerged."

But not even the quote could get rid of the bad taste in his mouth.

It happened like this: After a dusty tour of the commercial district of Santa Ana with Merenciano and Luix Lómax, "just to take a look-see" and on Blind Man's recommendation, he had stopped by the office for a bit and from there, along with the popular Canales, broadcaster of Radio Santa Ana, and his assistant, he had gone to eat at a tavern.

"I read all your novels, chief," Canales had told him.

"I hear that every day," José Daniel had answered.

"No one cares, you're hostage to the public."

"Breaded steak with lots of potatoes," said Barrientos.

"And how does it work, that new radio system you're putting up? Sometimes you hear it all over town and sometimes it's turned off."

"It's a stab at the limits of democracy," said the thin, eternally optimistic Canales. "You think if someone wants to hear, they turn it on and that's that. We don't have to force you to hear, but sometimes it's important to communicate with the whole town, so then the radio goes public, obligatory, in the streets; that's why we connected that system of loudspeakers. Now we're just testing, that's why you wake up to *boleros* by José Feliciano and when you're just at the point of solving a crime, you have to do it with the farm news at full volume . . . But it won't be so bad . . . I have millions of ideas. Start off Sundays with Tchaikovsky's *1812* Overture at full blast, cannons included. Public serenades to beatified mothers, once in a while news of a famous Priísta arrested for adulterating milk or raping his niece . . . Can you imagine? One hundred sixteen speakers telling that story. Son of a bitch . . ."

Canales got dreamy with the Hollywood perspective drifting through his head.

"It also serves to call for help in case of fire, or to pass on organizational slogans, or for . . ." Barrientos had said, in a more practical vein.

"No need to abuse it," José Daniel had recommended, thinking of Orwell's Big Brother.

"Abuse is when you turn on the TV and there's only bullshit," Canales had replied.

"Exactly," replied JD.

The tavern only had four tables, and the food was so home-made you could see it cooking on the hearth from the middle of the counter. There were no tricks; you simply decided and if you wanted the steak with onions, you pointed and they put it on the charcoal grill.

Canales got up and went to the fridge for beer.

JD smoked, watching the street. He witnessed the arrival of the two guys with shotguns, jumped up from the table and went running to the only safe place in the tavern, the bathroom. He would never remember if he screamed or if the cry remained locked up inside him. He heard the blast, and felt the scattered shot that searched him out, blowing apart a hardware store calendar featuring a big-assed blonde whose head was twisted oddly to look at the camera.

Of the three, maybe Canales, returning with the three beers in one hand, had the best view. He saw JD jump up and flee to the bathroom, caught a brief glimpse of the guy with the shotgun, and managed to see Blind Man under the overturned table shooting toward the entrance. He saw how the bullets hit one of the gunmen in the face, blowing his hat back. He saw how the second fled, firing into the air to make room, to comfort himself, to give himself courage.

When JD stuck his head out, Blind Man Barrientos was kicking the dead man's shotgun away, so the faceless corpse could not twitch and press the trigger in death.

For a moment, silence settled on the little tavern, broken only by the meat hissing on the fire, and the noise of the street.

The other patrons, a pair of campesinos, had not had time to figure out what was going on, and now contemplated the stars of the drama with admiration.

"What happened, chief?" asked Blind Man without looking at José Daniel.

"What the fuck do you think happened, asshole?"

"I don't know, suddenly you were there and just as suddenly you weren't, like the magician Chen-kai. You disappear very prettily."

JD vacillated between answering, hiding his head under his wing, instantly resigning his post as chief of police of Santa Ana, or going back to the bathroom. It wasn't clear which was more dangerous, the guys with the shotgun or Blind Man's sarcasm.

"What speed!" said Blind Man, loading the clip of the .45 with bullets from his pocket.

"Okay, okay, I warned you. And what was I going to

respond with, my fork?'' he had asked, holding up his knife and fork.

"Canales, call the Red Cross to come get the stiff."

"Who is he?" asked JD.

"Nobody from around here," replied Blind Man.

15.

Dear Ana/April 16

~~~~~~

Dear Ana/April 16
This is . . . like life itself.
I shall abandon literature to dedicate myself to writing the words to *boleros*. Everything's clear.
Absolute fucking life itself.
And I didn't know until now.
I love you as always and a bit more because distance works miracles on marriage, José Daniel, alias "Chief Fierro."

16.

Daylight Photo and Rotten Meat

＊＊＊＊＊＊＊＊＊＊＊＊＊＊＊＊＊＊＊＊＊＊

"I heard they shot at you yesterday."

"I ran like hell."

"That's how it's done, chief, we can't let them kill us. And you know what, I didn't think they'd allow it either," said Mayor Benjamín Correa to José Daniel Fierro, while they moved to the wall to form up with the rest of the municipal cops of Santa Ana for the photo.

"Maybe they didn't shoot to kill," replied JD, "but nobody told me."

"And how do you feel?"

"Like shit . . . It's never happened to you?"

"Experience doesn't help. Every time they shoot at you is like the first time."

"Close in," said the photographer.

José Daniel put his arm on Blind Man Barrientos's shoulders; he had taken his hat off so his face would show up well in the photo.

"So, Benjamín, do we get a new patrol car?" asked Popochas, legally registered in Santa Ana as Luix Lómax.

"You've got something better, shitface, the best town in Mexico under your care."

"All right then," said Merenciano, who posed with his .45 in hand and leaning a bit to one side.

The photographer, hidden behind his old tripod camera, scolded:

"Now shut the fuck up, or you'll all come out with your mouths crooked."

"Your ass is crooked," shouted Lómax.

"Can you prove it, motherfucker?" asked the photographer, ready to interrupt his work to beat up the cop.

"Calm down, Señor Photographer, sir, you'll get three days in jail for striking a police officer in uniform," said JD.

"Shut that guy up, chief," replied the photographer, pointing to Lómax with his finger.

"Popochas, control yourself."

"Whatever you say, chief."

It was still early and you could hear the sparrows and footsteps in the street. The six cops and the mayor stayed still and smiled for an instant. The flash never went off, only the click.

"Another," ordered the photographer.

"Go," said Benjamín Correa.

In the office half an hour later, José Daniel Fierro discovered that he could see a tree from his window, just as he could from his window in Mexico City. It was not a laurel but an ocote, but it was a tree.

"Does it have birds?"

"What?" asked Blind Man.

"The tree across the street."

"It must have, that's what it's for, isn't it?"

JD wanted to write down his assistant's words.

Merenciano came in leading an old woman by the hand.

She was radiant, very dark, with two braids held with red cords in hair turning gray, dressed in blue percale.

"Chief, my mother says they're selling rotten meat in the butcher shop run by the honcho of the CTM."

JD got up, giving a furtive glance at the tree.

"Who's in charge of such things in the government?"

"We have a veterinary student two doors down."

"Bring him here in a flash, Assistant Barrientos."

"Shit, the way things move around here."

17.

Dear Ana/April 17

Dear Ana/April 17

So that there's a record of my people somewhere there in Mexico City, I send a photocopy of the payroll list (in case nobody wants to believe me) and a photo (I'm the one in the middle). With guys like these and Spitfires, Churchill could have won the Battle of England in one and a half months.

• Barrientos, alias "Blind Man," my assistant chief, former taxi driver, wonderful marksman, future bigamist, lover of poetry, participates in a literary workshop with Canales at midnight, Tuesdays and Thursdays, in a bar.

• Luix Lómax, alias "Popochas." Studies law by correspondence school. Changed his name legally. Childhood polio, limps with his right leg, from Guanajuato. Subchampion in the fifty-yard dash in the mini-Olympics for the handicapped. (I'm serious! Look in the *Ovaciones* newspaper of May 1980 if you don't believe me.)

• Marcelo (no last name whatsoever), alias "Greñas," former insurance salesman, born in Santa Ana. Gets red in the face at times of crisis. I have found no medical explanation among the local eminences for this phenomenon.

• Merenciano, alias "With Mouth and Hand." Gossips say he is an ace at masturbation. Silent. Goes around town on a motorcycle. When I ask him a question, he answers with another. Was a bartender. The owner threw him out when he refused to water the drinks.

• Martín Morales, alias "the Russian." Teachers' union activist from the early days. A year ago the judicial police kidnapped him and beat him for two days to make him sign a false confession involving our mayor. He didn't sign a fucking thing.

The biggest scientific advance I've made in a week was to organize, at Marcelo's suggestion, an interpolice tournament of dominos by pairs.

Isn't it wonderful?

I adore you. JD

18.

Notes for the History of the Radical City Government of
Santa Ana
José Daniel Fierro

◥◣◥◣◥◣◥◣◥◣◥◣◥◣◥◣◥◣◥◣◥◣◥◣◥◣◥◣◥◣◥◣

Tape recording made with Mario Lapiedra Cruz, shopkeeper.
   "I arrived here in 1959, after two weeks in jail at Matías
Romero, with the railroad workers. I was assistant to the
telegraphist in the days of the movement and affiliated with
the Mexican Workers Communist Party . . . sixteen pesos
for bread, sweetheart . . . And I was on the run from that
but my ideas were still firm, moreover I had a few pennies
inherited from the wife's dad, now dead, both of them, my
wife and her dad, and so I set up the store. See? Outside you
see written "The Winner," the lettering is from back then,
because I didn't want to keep tasting the beating they had
given us, and so I put "The Winner" in red letters with black
trim. No, the black trim very light, so no one would see it
was a flag, and to disguise it I painted two bulls, one on each
side of the sign, but if you look hard you'll see the horns on

the left are bigger . . . Leave it, I'll weigh it, the melon is very good, sir . . . You see the sign outside, it's old now, right? Like me, but I haven't changed it, it's from the old days. So I came and opened the store, with a boy who went north later on, his name was Isaías, religious, one of those guys who pray all night long, son of a bitch, okay. And I stayed quiet in 1959, in 1960, in 1961, in 1962. So quiet that if you had seen me then you'd have said that guy is a complete sissy. A fag. But I was waiting. In 1963, the leftist Presidential candidate passed by on tour and I approached him at the hotel and said: You take down the address of a supporter, Mario Lapiedra, and when you need me, send for me. He never sent word, he must have thought I was just a big mouth, and there you have it, quiet for another twelve years. And sometimes I said to myself: Something has to happen in this town, here or somewhere else. But it made me mad not knowing what to do. So I felt like climbing a ladder and changing the name of the store to ''The Pussy'' but then I would not only be a failure but left without customers too. So I contained myself, for that and because my wife had been sick since 1971. Until in 1982, when Benjamín arrived and said to me: They tell me you were a Vallejista. And I told him, 'Now is the time.' . . . Grapes at eight hundred pesos, sweetie.''

19.

At Fifty Yards

At fifty yards José Daniel Fierro appears an ungainly character who miraculously broke through the barrier of silent film to arrive alone and desperate in the commercial cinema of the 1960s: movies about drug running on the border and so on.

At fifty yards, the house where 153 kilos of marijuana were being guarded looked neither like the House of Usher nor the pantheon of that celebrated Mexico City chief of police in the middle of the 1980s. At fifty yards it looked more like a white mansion surrounded by roses, for a bucolic film with Jorge Negrete and a few grande dames of Mexican movies.

Nor was it clear at the same fifty yards if the man seated in the rocking chair with the shotgun in his arms was alert, dead, or asleep. But Blind Man with his glasses of fifteen diopters sees more than the eye of God and he indicates with humility:

"No, chief, he's smoking."

"He wouldn't be farting by any chance?" asked JD, cowering on the ground and trying to see more than was possible through the bushes.

"Farts don't smoke," responded his assistant, carefully hidden near the same bush, but with a stone between him and the shotgun of the man seated in the rocking chair.

"You who see everything, Blind Man, tell me if our forces are now in place."

"Popochas just arrived, limping, he's maybe twenty yards in back of us, and Merenciano is settling in behind the gate."

"Then let's go, I want to smoke a cigarette too," says José Daniel Fierro, who still does not get up because he does not want to be shot.

"We'll drag ourselves out there and take off his shoes?" asks Blind Man, who has made enormous advances in sarcasm these last few days.

"It's just that it strikes me as ridiculous to shout 'You're surrounded,' " says the chief of police of Santa Ana, excusing himself.

"You're the writer, say something far out."

But José Daniel Fierro couldn't think of anything memorable.

At fifty yards you wouldn't know if the man in the rocking chair smiles or suffers from pancreatic colic. And José Daniel Fierro thinks that, fortunately, at fifty yards the man couldn't see how yellow he was either. So he gets on his knees and cries, "Surrounded!"

Which must have been interpreted by the man in the rocking chair as "Impounded," and seeing a man on his knees at fifty yards, does not know what to watch, nor what is being impounded, nor what he's supposed to do, except to get on his feet and aim.

Fortunately, the act of aiming is interpreted by Merenciano as a direct assault on the recently inaugurated chief of police of Santa Ana, and an invitation to shoot the guy in the thigh with a bullet from a .22 rifle, because it's the only one he's got, and the guy in the rocking chair lets go of his shotgun and curses the fucking mother of the marksman who caught him unawares.

A cat comes out the front door of the house, and then a few minutes later a woman with nothing on but a tiny pair of panties, whose breasts sway from east to west, provoking Blind Man to distraction so that he doesn't see the machine gun barrel poke out the second-story window.

So it goes, and when the first burst of fire raises dirt near José Daniel Fierro's bush, Blind Man doesn't know if the one with big tits fired from her two powerful nipples or if someone else is trying to get them out of the game, and while he figures it out, he throws himself behind the rock and opens fire with his .45.

José Daniel Fierro feels like he's pissing and he is in fact pissing. Terror invades and paralyzes him and the dirt flies around him.

Blind Man, in front, his back to him, takes up firing position and lets loose at the window with the whole clip of his .45, one after another, although after the third there's no one in the window, just his shots breaking the silence. With the seventh he gets up, José Daniel follows, feeling his knee joints creak and his kidneys hurt, with a stinging pain that diminishes little by little as his fear gives way.

At fifty yards, Merenciano and Popochas advance on the house with their eyes wide open, measuring every step, but there is only silence.

"Is it over?" José Daniel asks his assistant.

"I guess so," he says, shaking off the dust without turning around, leaving his chief time to recover his presence of mind.

"Good, because if they start shooting again I won't be able to piss anymore," says Chief Fierro, smiling, because he knows that fear does not define a man, but sincerity does.

20.

No Way

![decorative rule]

He let himself fall, bouncing on the mattress, without taking his boots off. He hurt from the hair on his head to the toes of his feet. He would not be able to sleep. He had never been able to sleep when he was tired. He should get up, take a hot shower and two aspirins, drink two cognacs, listen to Schubert. I won't sleep, he said to himself, tracing the lines drawn on the ceiling with his eyes.

He caught a movement from the door to the bathroom and immediately looked for the shotgun he had left in a corner of the room. A woman's voice aborted the planned leap from the bed.

"Steady now, little friend, I didn't come to hurt you, just to make you happy."

She was young, a fair-skinned brunette, with long loose black hair that fell to a strapless red dress, sewn onto her flesh by a skilled seamstress. A whore from the Mexican cinema of the 1950s. Even the way she talked.

The woman slid to the bed. She walked with difficulty because her dress was so tight it made her move her legs like the arms of a compass of short arc.

"Just relax and let go."

"Miss, I need your name."

"María, my dear."

"Okay, María, who sent you?"

"I came by myself, as a favor to the city. I try out all the important visitors who come here."

"What strange traditions remain in the provinces."

María lifted her arms to her back looking for the zipper. José Daniel felt tempted to help her. For reasons that were not strictly erotic, simply because it hurt him to see her sewn up so tight. He controlled himself. In high school, way back in 1947, a Basque professor of his, named Belascoarán, had instilled in him the sage maxim that he should not go putting his dick into women he didn't know. Advice as hard to defend as the rights of an author.

As the whole world knows, sex is a chain of reactions that begins with noises (a zipper running, the whisper of silk, a strangled sigh, a little cry muffled by a pillow between the teeth) that travel to the brain, which sends signals to the penis. All of this would be under control if one were deaf, but JD was not.

The woman stood up and let the dress slide over her body. Obviously she had nothing on underneath. The nipples of her two full breasts stared at José Daniel. A twinge reminded him of his headache and he narrowed his eyes. The woman interpreted his gesture as disgust.

"Don't you like them, papacito?"

She advanced toward the bed, to the post on the headboard, and began to masturbate. Her breasts knocked on the metal, swaying the mattress.

Obviously she wants to fuck, thought José Daniel in a last attempt to maintain his lucidity. Who? Why? The woman moved the mattress to and fro, knocking the slats of the bed with her pubis and staring at him.

José Daniel got up and went for the shotgun. He cocked it.

"Don't play with that, papacito, just take off your clothes instead."

José Daniel aimed at the woman's navel to avoid temptation.

"Who sent you, María? I'm giving you one minute to answer me. If you don't say, I'll shoot your leg and say you tried to kill me with a razor blade. You'll see yourself in hell with that red dress and crotch."

"What a bad boy you are."

"You've got thirty seconds left . . . I'll count them for you . . . twenty-nine . . . twenty-eight . . ."

"Don Sabás sent me, but not for anything bad. He just told me, fuck him. That's all. Nothing's going on. It was in good faith."

José Daniel gestured with the shotgun, indicating the door. "Out."

"Now be good. Just let me get dressed."

"Nope. As you are," said the chief of police of Santa Ana, planting a boot on the red dress.

The woman backed out with her eyes on the shotgun. Then she turned and fled the room.

José Daniel, hypnotized, watched the pair of swaying buttocks that fled their destiny. "What a chump," he said of himself.

He picked up the phone. Dialed five numbers.

"Greñas? . . . Do you know where Don Sabás lives? . . . There's a naked woman in the hallway of my hotel, a whore whom I believe is named María. Arrest her on morals charges, and take her to Don Sabás . . . That's what I said . . . Are you married? . . . Better yet . . . Take her to the front door and tell them that the chief of police ordered she be delivered there, because the lady gave that as her address . . . Exactly."

He hung up, advanced to the door and pushed an armchair against it. Then returned to bed and fell on the mattress. He passed his hand across his face and dried the sweat. Now he would be able to sleep. But he would sleep badly.

Six hours later he was awakened by a knock on the door. The sun was pouring in the window.

"Chief, there's a rumor going around town that you're a fag," announced Blind Man Barrientos, opening the door and sticking his head into the room.

José Daniel walked to the bathroom and carefully washed his face.

"What's to be done?"

"It's a blot on the force. If we don't fix it, no one will have any respect for us, no matter how well armed we are and even though we buy a new squad car."

"I can show the whole world a photo of my grandchild," said José Daniel while he dried his face.

"It won't work, chief."

"Then what?"

"Right this minute we're going to the whores, you and me. With the union Canales organized the other day. They're our very own."

"No way," said José Daniel.

21.

Dear Ana/April 18

Dear Ana/April 18
Today, I'd better not tell you anything.
But I love you.

JD

22.

Science

"Lómax, repeat," said JD, leaning on the omniscient chalk-board, which was full of schemes that were at this height incomprehensible.

"Half an hour before, go over the road they're coming in on and check all the rooftops."

"Barrientos?"

"Maintain a volunteer guard . . ."

"Of helpers called the Baker Street Irregulars."

"Of kids, then. Put the kids in front of the offices of the state judiciary and let them whistle if they see any strange movement."

"Define 'strange movement.' "

"More than one person leaving with a long weapon."

"Morales, alias the Russian?"

"Watch the main street with a walkie-talkie and if a car turns off toward the highway too quickly, advise Barrientos."

"Barrientos?"

"If he tells me to, I close the street with the patrol car and announce it on the radio."

"Merenciano?"

"Check out the cathedral and then the portals and then station myself in the window over the stage."

"Greñas?"

"I block Calle Siete with a barrier, and don't let any demonstration pass that comes out of the PRI office."

"And if there's a lot of them and they're armed?"

"I advise Blind Man."

"Chief, one question."

"Spit it out."

"What if everything happens at the same time?"

"Everyone look to his saint."

"And where will you be?"

"Everywhere, like Spiderman."

Lómax controlled himself.

"That's not how we did it before," said Merenciano.

"And how did you do it before?" asked JD, ready to learn from the mistakes of others.

"Before we marched in the front with arms."

"That's not scientific," said JD. "Demonstrations have to be scientifically cared for. We are the armed force of popular power."

"That sounds like hot shit, chief, but let's hope there's no gunfire," said Blind Man.

"Amen," answered José Daniel.

23.

Riders in the Sky

"**A**nd you, why are you with the left?"

"Because in a former life I was on the right and my conscience shit on me."

"No, seriously."

"Let's see," said José Daniel Fierro, scratching his moustache with the barrel of his new shotgun, a tic that Blind Man deplored as being unprofessional. "With what they throw out in the garbage in Queens, New York, in one night, you could furnish a street in Cuzco ten thousand times better than it is now. With the leftovers from one middle-class restaurant in Caracas, sixty Algerian families could eat for five days. The bachelors who go out at night in Buenos Aires could delight all the single women who dream lonely dreams watching the stars of Bangkok. The books I've bought and not read would solve the problems of a middle school library in Camagüey. With the monthly salary of a trolley car driver in Mexico

City, you could live for one day at Caesars Palace in Las
Vegas. With the speeches of a PRI governor of Mexico, you
could drive six lie detectors crazy. With the fire that's in the
poems of Vallejo you could cook all the hot dogs consumed
in one day in Monterrey. All the words I've used over the
last thirty-five years to explain it, if they were stones, could
be used to construct the three pyramids of Cheops in Texcoco
. . . Do I make myself clear?"

"Would you repeat that for the tape recorder?" asked
Canales seriously.

"It never comes out the same."

Canales moved the button that disconnected the turntable
spitting out revolutionary corridos and went on live.

"Here, at XELL, Radio Santa Ana, the solitary red star
on your dial, broadcasting for insomniacs and middle school
students who are studying for their literature exams . . . And
for them, especially for them, a bit of music by Glenn Miller,
and let me remind you not to buy meat from La Favorita. It
is being boycotted by the Popular Organization."

He hit the switch and connected the second turntable.

"How do you know about the middle school?"

"They are my students, they have an exam tomorrow,"
said Canales, smiling.

"What kind of batteries do you use, Canales? Mine give
out with the heat."

Without answering Canales walked to an icebox, the kind
only miserable lunchrooms could afford, and took out two
soft drinks that dripped freezing water.

"I never imagined myself broadcasting with a novelist
here, live, at midnight."

"Novelists don't sleep in Santa Ana."

"You'd be surprised how many people don't sleep. These
fucking people have insomnia since we won the elections.
Just dreams and nightmares, neighbors."

José Daniel smiled.

"I'm sleeping badly."

"I haven't slept for two months," said Canales, very seriously.

"Really?"

"Really, ask Fritz . . . Have you ever been a member of a political party?"

"I joined the Communist Party in 1959. Until 1962. I left with Revueltas. Then I went it alone, without a party. In 1969 I was about to go out to the country, with a group that was organizing communal lands in Veracruz. I suppose I could continue being left-wing for that. Because the organized left didn't consume me the way it did so many others . . . I've seen the best minds of my generation getting paid by the treasury."

"And before you were a writer?"

"There was no before. When I was nine years old I knew."

"But your first book came out in 1964. You were twenty-nine then."

"I was late in getting clear on what I wanted to write about. For a third worldist who wants to eat the novel with the novel, who thinks that fame and glory depend on his capacity to enchant the metropolis, that is, to fool it, to put fear into his own pen, to darken the text so it appears absolutely transcendent, it is hard to arrive at the conclusion that what I really always wanted to write is a good adventure story. A kind of realism/social realism/adventure, which is not realism, is half socialist, and is completely an adventure. It was hard. While I got that clear, I worked as the manager of a supermarket, an editor, a professor of English literature, an assistant theatrical director, and a commissioned salesman for a rum manufacturer."

Canales stared at him for a moment, then returned to his console.

"And now, for those who are almost asleep, and dedicated to the managers of supermarkets, who if they pressure their consciences a bit will end up being writers of detective novels, 'Riders in the Sky.' "

"Aren't you driving people crazy?"

"They're used to it," said Canales, smiling as his long skinny crossed legs followed the rhythm of the march that sounded like a Western.

24.

Dear Ana/April 19

Dear Ana/April 19
If you're going to divorce me, for God's sake send me the
blue turtleneck sweater and the aspirins, Manchette's novels,
the three books by Rodolfo Walsh held by a rubber band that
were on top of the table, the draft of the novel that is in the
green folder, the one that says "New Lies," the gray suede
boots, the photo of my nephews pissing that I have in the
bookcase on the right, the three green notebooks of notes that
are in the drawer at the left of the desk, the yellow fountain
pen and its cartridges, a novel by Roger Simon (*The Straight
Man*) that's in the bookcase in the hall, the dark glasses I
kept in the sewing kit, a pair of black corduroy pants, old,
with patches on the knees, two boxes of Maalox (you, you're
constipated, you don't ever use it), the correspondence with
the Strugatski brothers, in a folder under S in the file cabinet,
my old address book, the photo of Argel's grandfather (and
don't take it out of the frame, okay?), the medium chess set,

a cloak-and-dagger novel by Shellabarger that must be under the bed, volume two of *Les Misérables* by Victor Hugo (you'll find it easily, it has a red spine, bound in leather), the box of French paper that's under the desk, and the book of Benedetti's poems, with dedication.

If you've got any time left, send me the last photo of us together.

All this if you're going to divorce me. If you're not, send it all anyway, I'll be even more grateful.

　　　　　　　　　　　　　　　JD, who still loves you.

25.

Flowers in the Plaza

━━━▲▲▲▲▲▲▲▲▲▲▲▲▲▲▲▲▲▲━━━

For José Daniel, the morning of April 20 began when he looked out the window of his hotel room and a worker for the soft drink bottler let a handful of dahlias fall on the sidewalk at the corner of Benito Juárez. Moments later, there were three or four market women carrying gladiolas. Then close to two hundred children from the middle school with daisies, which they dropped to the ground, as if carelessly, covering the place where Doña Jerónima had been killed four years ago.

José Daniel washed his face carefully, with cold water, which made his skin throb as if it were burning.

He walked out the door of the Hotel Florida. The loud-speakers connected to Radio Santa Ana repeated a song by Silvio Rodríguez, oddly cadenced in waltz time. A song whose chorus repeated: "I know you."

JD walked on, striking the tips of his mining boots on the

paving stones. Turning the corner to the portals, he met the lawyer Mercado with a wreath of roses in his hand.

"Want one?"

"Thank you," said JD with a timid smile.

They walked together in silence to the street corner.

The pavement was covered with flowers, and from every corner of the plaza came men and women, children, elders, the ugly, the tall, the beautiful enough to drive you mad with their total splendor, those confused by morning and faraway memories, by the music that blared from the loudspeakers and raised their moustache hairs, the smiles, the recently combed hair, the drops of morning dew between their teeth.

José Daniel Fierro let his rose fall amid the rest of the flowers. And assumed the ritual silence, the felt end to the act. Now, he was one neighbor more in Santa Ana. Their dead were his dead.

26.

You Really Don't Like It?

━━━━━━━━━━━━━━━━━━━━━━━━━━━━━━━

His police were transformed. The silent Martín Morales, alias the Russian, howled the rhythmic "Popular power, popular power" with his face bright red; the nose of Marcelo—Greñas—broke the air inches before its owner's face like an icepick, leading forth a character full of security. With a gesture, JD reminded them to occupy their designated places. They retired in protest.

JD found Carlos Monsiváis in the fourth line of the demonstrators advancing toward City Hall, at the edge of the crowd, a bit alien, looking at everything he could without appearing to stare.

"I know you recommended me to this infamous post. You're a fucking traitor."

"You really don't like it?"

"I love it. Aside from being shot at twice, and one of those times I peed my pants, I love it."

"Then I was right," said the other writer.

JD lifted two fingers to the visor of his baseball cap and moved on. He looked toward the rooftops of the buildings searching for nonexistent sharpshooters. He was here in his role as chief of police, not narrator. He saw other things. He could leave for another day the careful observation of women in red and green aprons, armed with posters and wreaths of flowers, who lifted their fists half high as if they still maintained some hint of shame. It was not an orderly demonstration. Miners and farmers, squads of the Popular Organization, elementary school teachers, women from the neighborhood committees, members of the reborn prostitutes' union (two arm in arm with the tall Canales), taxi drivers and small business owners, middle school students, many farmers, workers from the soda pop and gypsum factories, marching all mixed together, some with their own posters in which the spirit was stronger than the spelling.

Entering the plaza he saw Merenciano with his shotgun in the window of City Hall above the stage. When the first contingents began to turn the corner into the plaza, all the loudspeakers surged with the first chords of Beethoven's Fifth. Canales winked at the police chief.

And thus Beethoven and forty thousand citizens of Santa Ana entered the plaza of their city on the 20th of April.

27.

Notes for the History of the Radical City Government of
Santa Ana
José Daniel Fierro

▬▬▬▬▬▬▬▬▬▬▬▬▬▬▬▬▬▬▬▬▬▬

The leadership of the Popular Organization does not agree
on an interpretation of what is happening. While Benjamín
believes in closing the circle and that the key moment will
be within the next six months, before the towns destroy the
PRI dominance in the whole region (at least in the other
six towns that advance stubbornly following Santa Ana's
example), Mercado believes that something strange is happening now, and the leaders of the miners' unions think that
the enemy is in retreat and now is the hour to advance.

We are almost speaking of a problem raised by a game of
divination. In one matter we are all in agreement, the state
apparatus has remained without support in Santa Ana and
will have to bring in outside help or break the PO's unity to
give itself room. Blind Man says this is the hour of the
traitors, but that they must have made themselves scarce.

Benjamín, meanwhile, has elaborated a theory of siege. Basically, he means to oppose the pressure (economic: they hold back city funds collected in taxes by the state government, anticipated federal funds don't arrive, traditional federal support is diverted to other regions: bank loans, highways, public health clinics under construction, publicity, sanitation) with a pressure from inside consolidating the power of the radical city government and extending it to the neighboring zones, gently and cautiously, and with another, external, pressure: a national publicity campaign involving intellectuals, journalists, artists, and even the few left-wing deputies in parliament.

This is what I'm here for, I have no illusions. I'm lending my name to the revolution: the impossible and for that not any less necessary revolution. The difference between me and other writers and journalists who are jumping into the struggle with both feet at the call of the radical city government is that I don't write a thing, and nevertheless, I play at the statues of salt while I walk through town in my uniform and baseball cap.

Whatever comes out of it, it's certain that Benjamín's tactic is getting results, the name Santa Ana is beginning to take on national and even international fame thanks to the foreign press and translations of the Mexican press in French and American magazines.

No doubt the attraction of Santa Ana is the unanimity it presents, the nonexistence of cracks in its justice on the one hand, and two complementary factors on the other. The first has to do with the pride of victory that everyone takes on by extension, in a country that makes us all minorities despite ourselves, that condemns the timid to silence and the daring to isolation. The second is visual: there are no beggars in Santa Ana. Our miracle was not that we extracted petroleum where there was none to be found, but that we have won back the most important human resource in this country: the hundreds of children who work from the age of five selling gum and newspapers, the women who stretch out their hands, the men who sell Kleenex without looking you in the eye. The child care centers, the shelters, the municipal employment plan, the cooperative stores, and above all the legion of voluntary social workers who have thrown themselves on the streets to reconstruct the human landscape, have achieved a great victory.

These are overwhelming arguments for organizing solidarity around Santa Ana, but do nothing to brake the offensive of its enemies.

28.

Dear Ana/April 20

Dear Ana/April 20
  Before you say fifty-two years old, I say nearly fifty-two, and each year is one more in a line, waking you up in the middle of a dream to say I'm an asshole, I should dedicate myself to arithmetic, I don't know how to write, how could anyone be so imbecilic, so absolutely conceited as to have once believed himself master of words and sentences, speeches and paragraphs, entire chapters, when he is really master of nothing, not even the Olivetti Lettera 25 I beat on, or the paper, or the commas in the wrong place and another job before tears flow from my eyes and another fucking job in which the dance from euphoria to depression is not calisthenic, toboggan-like, the leap from the Latin American Tower to the ground in ten seconds; and I tell you that while you cover your head and say it will pass, as if it were the slogan of the Spanish Civil War, *no pasarán,* but it does not pass and goes on at my side accompanying me, the faithful

mark of the job the fear of words that don't exist, sentences that say the opposite, inchoate ideas, uncapturable landscapes, erratic characters, vagabond plots, wounded to death, and fuck the book, which then falls from the hands because no fragrance of ink or sentence makes the nightmare a dream and from the dream the tranquillity that comes from finishing the final touches, although later I must correct them a thousand times and the best novel is that which is never finished, is never written, but always thought of, the one carried inside forever that will die with you because of that absurd marriage between the book that will never come about and the man who will never write it.

And who can I tell this to? Because the mirror already warned me it won't take another fucking monologue for depressed assholes.

For you, of course.

I love you: JD

29.

Birds

From the window of his room in the Hotel Florida, José Daniel Fierro watched the swarms of thrushes drawing circles in the sky of Santa Ana, crazy gyrations, absurd turns, writing a message in the air that could not be retained . . . They come nineteen miles from González Ortega to sleep in Santa Ana. They eat in the wheat fields of the cañadas and at dusk fly to Santa Ana to fill the laurels of the plaza, shit on pairs of sweethearts, and after warbling an hour and making the trees appear like live, irritated, and palpitating masses of green, they sleep in the city. How far is nineteen miles to a bird? Far? Maybe a bit less, because it is nineteen miles on the highway, and the birds fly in a straight line. Why do they sleep here? For the same reason I do?

The lights of the town begin to go on. José Daniel dries his sweat with a bandana and watches the patrol car pass down below, driven by the Russian, who accompanies Merenciano.

On the little table by the window, an open bottle of brandy

stood alongside the typewriter. The only glass was dirty, muddy with cigarette butts tossed in the night before. The birds were disappearing from the sky and he drank from the bottle.

This is the worst hour in Santa Ana, the moment of solitude before he decides to write a bit or listen to music stretched out in bed, or until someone appears to offer a last nocturnal round through town, filling the mortal hour with old stories that to JD appear eternally new, freshly unveiled.

The telephone rang. JD smiled at the apparatus, which guessed at his solitude.

"We have a bizarre death, chief," said Barrientos's voice in his ear.

"Why?"

"You'll see. Come downstairs and I'll be there on the bike in two minutes."

JD hung up and dried his face again. The sky was clean of birds, the last lights were on. The street was, nevertheless, deserted. "They must all be shitting," as Merenciano says when the streets suddenly empty at certain hours of the afternoon and the city dozes among the sounds of creaking bedsprings.

His baseball cap lay on the bed. JD put it on and adjusted it in the mirror, which showed a grim and sullen look.

30.

Candles in Church

~~~~~~

JDF made his way through the women in mourning, the butcher with his deliveries on the back of his bicycle, two altar boys. The church was dark, and smelled of damp and of rancid death, but the bloody woman was young, the naked body out of place in front of the altar. José Daniel tried to construct a literary image and words like "obscene" or "profane" did not appear, just flashes from pop art, plastic mannequins, Andy Warhol and European design magazines. The murdered woman was that unreal.

"Who is she?"

"I have no idea, chief. All she's got on is the knife she was killed with. The altar boy found her fifteen minutes ago and advised a cop going by," said Barrientos.

José Daniel approached the corpse and took the undone face between his hands, trying to avoid contact with the knife that stuck out from the center of her chest. She was young, blond, her hair fell over one eye in that hairstyle like Veronica

Lake that reminded him of a girlfriend he'd had when he studied in London, who looked at him with an intensity that came of using only one side of her face, the other appearing and disappearing in the soft sway of a short mane of hair. The blue eyes looked right through the chief of police of Santa Ana, looking at a killer who was now long gone. The body was still warm.

"Does anyone know her?" José Daniel asked Barrientos. Blind Man shook his head.

"Tell the Russian to come here. Get everyone together here, and bring me the altar boy who found her . . . Lómax! Find me Dr. Jiménez . . . I want to speak with the priest of this church, the earthly proprietor as he would say . . . Doesn't anyone know her?" he asked the spectators for the second time, raising his voice over the Santa Ana cops who were filing in and making a small protective barrier around their chief, ready to obey orders and make suggestions at the drop of a hat. With one theatrical gesture José Daniel made the bystanders, who were filling the church, move back a few paces. The cadaver was lying on the stairs that led to the altar, between the altar and a confessional of black wood.

"I'm the one who found her, Chief Fierro," said a disheveled altar boy who did not reach José Daniel's waist.

"I need more light, light all the candles."

"The señor priest doesn't like it."

"But I do, and this matter is for the Santa Ana police and not God, my child."

The church began to light up as the altar boy ran from one side to the other, touching fire to wick. The butcher and a lay sister began to help him. The body of the blond woman acquired a greater presence as the shadows retreated. It was becoming the center of a new rite that would be remembered years later as the-night-when-Chief-Fierro-found-the-dead-gringa.

"Greñas, come here and take a good look at this knife without touching it. Have you seen one before?"

"Everywhere, chief, they're butcher knives, or taco

knives. They sell them everywhere, even in the supermarket.''

"Here's the Russian," said Barrientos.

"Catch that altar boy and bring him here . . . Russian, station yourself in the doorway and let me know when the judicial police arrive.''

"Should I stop them?''

"No, just tell me.''

"Here he is, chief," said Barrientos.

"Okay, kid, how did you find her?''

"I came into the church and there was no one here, chief. And there'd been nobody else 'cept that dead blonde. I went running and called the butcher going by on his bike.''

"It was ten o'clock," said the butcher, coming forward. "I went outside and the patrol car went by and I shouted at them real loud.''

"And the priest?''

"He doesn't come today, it's his day to visit other towns in the district," said Blind Man.

"And what were you doing, little one, dressed as an altar boy?''

"Practicing, chief—him too," he said, pointing at the second altar boy a few feet away, clinging to a column with such strength that he appeared to be holding up the small temple.

"That's right," said the second witness.

"Thursdays at night we practice.''

"And the church is open even though the priest doesn't come?''

"Yes, it stays open, for anyone who needs it.''

"With or without lights?''

"I lit the bulb in the sacristy where I change clothes, chief.''

"Somebody must have seen you come in. Someone undressed her. They brought her dead or they killed her here, but to run around town with a naked blonde would provoke such a scandal that . . . Greñas!''

"He's in the doorway, chief."

"Assistant Barrientos, grab Greñas and interrogate everyone in the neighborhood, everyone who was hanging out in the doorway, taking a breath of fresh air, all the drunks, everyone on this and the next block. What are we looking for? A car that stopped in front of the church. A group of people with a woman along, two guys who carried a rug where a body would fit, someone who heard a cry, a quarrel, anything out of the ordinary . . ."

JD walks around the body as he continues to talk. He was out of character. He had entered a Mack Sennett comedy. Around the body, small pools of blood fall from the chest wound, one of them had been stepped in; you could barely see the print of a boot heel. He touches her again. She is still warm. As he lets the arm fall, he finds a one-inch tattoo in the interior of her forearm: a small rose with six words in English: Loneliness is the heart of life. Suddenly he wonders if the woman is a natural blonde and examines her roots. No signs of dye, she's blond and always has been.

"Dr. Jiménez!" cries Lómax, and enters running, holding the doctor by the arm.

"When did she die? Did a lefty strike the blow? Was she beaten? Was she raped? How old is she? Is that a new tattoo?"

Jiménez, a gray-haired man of some forty years, stares at Chief Fierro and smiles.

"This is the first instantaneous autopsy I've done in my life, chief. Everything I tell you will be a lie."

"Hurry, because we'll have the feds here any minute."

"I'll take a look, but don't worry. When they take the body, they'll take it to the morgue and the guy in charge there is Luis, who was my student in Durango . . . Just ask them to move back, I don't work in public."

JD steps back as an example and, at his gesture, the whispering crowd that fills the church moves back again. Those seated in the first rows go to the third, and so on, respecting the order of arrival.

"Does anyone know her?"

"You can't see from here," replies an old miner.

" 'Loneliness is the heart of life,' " José Daniel murmurs. "Lómax, have you ever taken fingerprints?"

Luix Lómax shakes his head.

"Does anyone have a Polaroid camera?"

"I do, chief," says one of the middle school teachers.

"Can you bring it?"

"I live far away."

"Lómax, take the teacher on the motorcycle and come right back. Do you have flash?"

The woman nods and smiles at the chief and Lómax.

" 'Fuenteovejuna against the Murderer of the Gringa,' they'll call the play," thinks José Daniel, who has tried to conduct the whole affair in the purest *procedural* style of the stories of McBain's 87th Precinct.

"She wasn't a virgin, doesn't appear to have been raped, she was killed half an hour ago or a little more, and I believe she died here because that's what the blood on the floor says, she died instantly. She has scratches on one arm and the neck, she could have been forced. I don't think she's thirty, but you never know. If she were a compatriot of mine from Durango, I could give her exact age, but she looks like a gringa or a rich girl from Polanco there in Mexico City," says Jiménez.

"How did you do it so well and so quickly?"

"I read all your novels, Chief Fierro."

"Son of a bitch," thought José Daniel, "that's how it goes."

"Cover her with a sheet!"

"Will a blanket do?" asked the butcher, who was of a literal bent.

JD nodded.

"Have you ever seen a knife like this one?"

"I have three of them" said the man, advancing toward the dead woman with a blanket passed up from the third row.

"Should I run the onlookers out of the church, chief?" asked Lómax.

"Why? The dead woman is just as much theirs as ours, they're not bothering anyone," answered José Daniel, who believes firmly in democratic police investigation.

The phrase "loneliness is the heart of life" reminds him of something he read once, but not in Spanish, in translation. Thomas Wolfe? Dylan Thomas? Someone like that.

"What time is it?"

"Fifteen to eleven, chief! Ten forty-eight!" respond the anonymous voices in chorus.

"Little one, what time did you find her?"

"I got here around ten-fifteen, chief."

"Russian, what time did the butcher call you?"

"A bit before ten-thirty, chief."

"Shit, they had just killed her, and here we were going over the business inside instead of following the fresh trail in the street. When I got here, twenty-five minutes hadn't gone by since the murder."

"I could be wrong and it was more like forty-five minutes," said Dr. Jiménez.

"No more than that?"

"No more, she was very warm, and the floor was cold."

José Daniel approached the body covered with a blanket and lifted a corner and the murmuring at his back increased. If he could only see the face without the traces of fear, of anguish, of tension from pain and the rigidity that death was beginning to imprint . . .

"Here's the teacher with the camera," says Lómax, dusty from driving the motorbike at sixty miles per hour in the streets of Santa Ana.

"Will you take them or should I?"

"Oh, no, chief, not me," said the teacher, passing him the camera and retreating a few yards.

"Uncover her, doc."

Slowly, JD begins to shoot photos of the body, the face from various angles, the position of the corpse, general shots. To see what comes out, more or less neatly.

"Here come the judicial police, chief," advises the child.

From the door, arms in hand, the chief of the group of state judicials comes in followed by two confederates in suits.

"Who killed her?" he asks, directing himself to Chief Fierro, who finished the roll in the Polaroid without looking up.

"Nobody here. She was found half an hour ago. No one knows anything or saw anything. Nobody knows her."

"The case is ours," says Durán Rocha.

Chief Fierro looks at him, trying to discover something, but sees only the scarred face of the cop.

"Let's go," he says to the doctor and Lómax, the Russian and Merenciano, but his voice is interpreted by the majority of the onlookers as a communal order, and the church begins to empty, to the judicials' surprise. The butcher puts out the candles as he leaves.

"The witnesses stay here!" says Durán Rocha but nobody pays any attention to him.

"You can come by tomorrow to read my report," answers Fierro, turning his back. The church empties, while the witnesses to the crime and the witnesses to the beginning of the investigation follow the police chief out to the street.

31.

Office Hours

"**P**ermission to go home and sleep is suspended until the investigation is over," said José Daniel, throwing the Polaroid shots on the table before a pair of agitated agents. "Take the motorcycle and hunt up Barrientos and Greñas; they're out doing investigations down the block and around the church, tell them the time of the crime was around ten at night, right there, in the church, the murderer and the blonde went in together, tell them she's probably gringa, tell them to look for her clothes, they must have been thrown away somewhere. Merenciano and the Russian should try the hotels with one of these photos. If you find the hotel where she was staying, call me, and then stand in the door to the room and don't let even a fly get in."

"What are you going to do, chief?"

"I'm going to make coffee. If I'm not here, I'll be at the broadcasting station. I saw a light on when we went by."

JD turned his back and went for the coffee pot. He didn't

know if he had them fooled, but he certainly had tried. Them and the whole town. If you give orders so rapidly that the guys who get them don't have time to think, it looks like the guy who's giving them knows what he's talking about. At least that's the way it looks and José Daniel in the role of Chief Fierro has convinced even himself. "What's missing?" he asked himself now in the empty office. He reviewed his arsenal of thirty-five years of reading detective literature: fingerprints, why, to identify her if she is a gringa, I suppose; put a tail on the judicials to see what they do, copies of the photos, what for?

José Daniel Fierro tips his baseball cap and serves himself the first of a long series of cups of coffee.

"Chief, an interview!" said long-legged Canales, entering the office and tripping over the coat rack.

"Do you know her, Canales?"

The skinny one looked at a photo of the dead woman's face, and then at the others.

"Son of a bitch, I saw her today."

"Where?"

"In Esther's bookstore, La Piedra Rodante."

"Who is she?"

"Who knows, but a Spanish-speaking gringa. She was chatting with Esther when I arrived to buy some books."

"What did you buy?"

"A new novel by Semionov."

"And where can we find Esther?"

"She lives above the bookstore . . . But first, an interview. Come to the station next door!"

"And who stays in the office?"

"Let's call Tomás, the night watchman. You give the instructions."

JD stopped. "Is there a way of tapping the judicials' phone?"

"We already have, it's just that we only have two shifts out of three, because not all the operators are with us. What do you want to know?"

"Everything. Who they talk to, about what."

"Wait a minute," said the skinny Canales and lifted the office telephone.

"María? Tell Laura to lend an ear she knows where, and if they call Chief Fierro, pass the calls on to the station, please; call Tomás at the entrance and tell him if the agents arrive to tell them the chief is at the station . . . All the above." Canales hung up and said to JD: "You owe me a supper, which is what it costs me for María to pass on three messages without forgetting anything."

JD walked alongside Canales. The night chilled the building's central patio. The radio station was empty, a revolving long-playing record of classical music and the red indicators on the switchboard were the only things stirring.

Canales took the microphone, threw a switch, and went on live.

"And here, from the broadcasting studios of Radio Santa Ana, a live interview with our chief of police, the famous writer José Daniel Fierro, who will review the facts of the strange murder perpetrated tonight in our city."

José Daniel got serious. Radio had the virtue of making him a character in a melodrama.

"At ten o'clock tonight a woman some twenty-five years old, blond, blue eyes, was murdered in the church on Calle Lerdo. The body was discovered minutes later by accident. She was found nude. She had been killed with a kitchen knife."

"Do you know the dead woman's name?"

"We still have no information, although we are investigating."

"Do you have any leads?"

"I reserve comment so as not to interfere with the investigation."

"Is it true that the judicial police arrived half an hour after you had begun the investigation?"

"That's true."

"Will the Santa Ana police be continuing their investigation of the murder?"

"Yes, although the judicial police are in charge, we will continue with our own investigation."

"Don't you have confidence in the state judicial police, Señor Chief of Police?"

"None at all. The crime occurred in our city, we were the first to discover the body, we will ascertain who killed the woman and why."

"Do you want the town's cooperation?"

"Yes, we're going to ask for various kinds of help. We urgently need to find out who the woman was, so we ask the inhabitants of Santa Ana, if they know or saw a woman who corresponds to the description, to report it immediately. We will put a photo of the body on the board at the entrance to City Hall to facilitate identification. We would also like to know if anyone saw anything out of the ordinary around ten at night near the church on Calle Lerdo. And since the woman was found naked, if a woman's clothing appears thrown out somewhere in town we would like to be informed immediately."

"Chief Fierro, are you asking the town to take up the investigation?"

"I certainly am. A woman died today, brutally murdered in our town. We are all responsible for finding the killers."

"Here, at Radio Santa Ana, live, you have just heard an interview with the city's chief of police, an hour after the murder committed in the Church of Carmen on Calle Lerdo . . . And now for you all, music of the Chilean resistance movement . . ."

Canales switched off the mike and brought up the music. "Do you have any ideas, chief?"

"I have a dead woman, and I take it as a personal offense."

"Against you?"

"Against her."

32.

Night Rounds

~~~~~~~~~~~~~~~~~~~~~~~~~~~

José Daniel lined up the four paper cups with the remains of coffee. It was his way of measuring the night. He began his report.

"If I'm wrong, if I skip things, if you don't understand me or if I don't understand me, cut me off, we'll discuss it and start over, as many times as we have to."

"We should interrupt you?" asked Merenciano.

"Exactly."

Around him, squeezed into school desks, the Russian and Merenciano, Blind Man Barrientos seated on the metal file cabinet, Lómax on the floor in lotus position, Canales standing in the door (in his capacity as connoisseur of the detective novel and not as broadcaster of Radio Santa Ana). The police force of the radical city government lit cigarettes and served themselves fresh cups of aromatic coffee.

"Yesterday afternoon, probably to attend the demonstration, or God knows why, a gringa arrived in town in a Renault

with California plates. She registered at Motel Lucas under
the name of Jessica Lange, which must be a pseudonym.''

"Jessica Lange, from *King Kong*?'' asked Canales.

"Exactly, but she isn't. Look at the photo, she's beautiful
but not that beautiful.''

"We didn't see her at the demonstration, but that means
nothing. At the motel she received no phone calls and all
they know is that she slept there and left again today in the
morning. The car isn't there, we know it's a red Renault but
don't know the plate numbers. Later we'll talk about that.''

"But the car was at the motel last night, or else she took
it out today,'' said the Russian.

"How did you know to search at a motel?'' asked Blind
Man.

"I didn't know, it just occurred to me.''

"That's called instinct,'' said Lómax.

"At the motel,'' continued José Daniel, "the room was
messy, there was no suitcase but some clothes were thrown
around, and a few other things: a Los Angeles newspaper
dated the eighteenth, a box of American chocolates, a novel
in English, a box of tampons and a toothbrush in the bathroom, two dirty changes of underwear near the shower, a
Zeiss telephoto lens that must have cost a fortune, a folder
with professional black and white photos, two-by-three stills,
all of a six- or seven-year-old boy. The folder had fallen
behind the mirror. The rest of the luggage was missing. We
know it was just one suitcase, of canvas, blue, because the
kid who waits on people who arrive there at night told us.
That's where we stand. All we've got left is the disappeared
car, the disappeared suitcase; we know she was in Los
Angeles two days ago, we know she registered under a false
name, that she left the motel today . . . We know that she
was at the bookstore. Tomorrow we'll follow up on that trail
. . . At ten o'clock she was dead and naked at the church.''

"Why naked?'' asked Barrientos.

"That's one of the clues. They took off her clothes because
there's something in them that could serve to identify her or

the murderers, or because they want to create a scandal with
a dead naked gringa in a church in Santa Ana.''

"Why the church?'' asked Barrientos again.

"One thing or the other. Either by accident, she was there
and they trapped her, or on the other hand . . .''

He paused, ritually, while everyone sipped their coffee.
Magnanimously he circulated a small flask of brandy that
came back to him empty.

"Shit, it was to flavor the coffee, not to drink coffee with
brandy to give it a better color . . . Okay. Somewhere near
Calle Lerdo, we still haven't found more than two clues.
Somebody saw a red car parked in front of the church, and
was at the point of telling them that the priest was away,
but . . .''

"Doña Lola,'' completed Greñas.

"Doña Lola had a sick kid and kept going. When she went
by the car was empty. When the altar boys found the body,
the car was gone. Two miners on the night shift brought us
some women's clothes that they found thrown in Avenida
Riva Palacio, behind a garbage can. With that we'll know if
they undressed her after they killed her . . . Nobody heard
anything else in the street.''

"We should go out again and start over,'' said Barrientos.
"We didn't talk to all the neighbors.''

"Okay, what do we have? A car. Everyone to the streets
to look for a gringo car with California plates. Not only here
in town, on the outskirts too. We'll cut the town in four and
divide it. Merenciano and Russian in the patrol car, take the
east and the north, Greñas on his bicycle, downtown which
is easier, Lómax the south with the motorcycle and follow
the outlying neighborhoods and the highways to Chihuahua
and Monterrey. Report back every fifteen minutes. Let's go.''

33.

Red Car Badly Parked

"**T**here's a time to ask questions . . . How would Pete Seeger say it, Canales?" said José Daniel, shadows under his eyes, lining up the nine paper cups.

"And a time to answer questions . . . Seeger according to Ecclesiastes," answered Canales from deep in an armchair. He did not know how to hide his excessively long legs.

Barrientos was still mounted on the file cabinet answering the telephone.

"This is not the time to ask questions. To ask a good question you have to know part of the answer. But still: What was she doing in church?"

"They killed her with her clothes on," said Barrientos, playing with the yellow dress they had brought in, its checked front bloody and torn by the knife. "First they killed her, then they undressed her."

"There was the print of a boot heel in the blood," said JD. And he began to draw it. "Just like this."

"Did you take a photo?"

"It didn't occur to me."

"I'll do it, chief."

"We'll do it tomorrow if the judicials haven't erased it . . . And nothing from that angle?"

Canales shook his head. "They called the capital once to report. They cursed you out various times, chief, for having gotten there first, but nothing else."

JD got up from his armchair and walked to the window. The streets were empty.

"What time is dawn here?"

"In half an hour," said Barrientos. And he stretched to answer the phone.

"Yes? Where?" Then, turning toward José Daniel, "They found the red car."

JD stretched, trying to touch the top of the window frame. He picked up his cap and the shotgun that hung behind the door.

"I'm going, the broadcast is about to start," said Canales. "I have a cot in the cabin. Do you want me to say anything more?"

"Give them a report on what happened last night."

Barrientos set out.

"How are we traveling?" asked JD, rubbing himself to shake off the cold.

"On the other motorcycle, the old one."

JD looked at the sky. The stars of Santa Ana had been out all week: thousands of them, burning like pale suns. His beard grew by the warmth of the stars. Blind Man revved the engine. JD got on the rear seat, hung the shotgun carefully on his back and cried, "Ready, Assistant Chief."

The motorbike took off like a shot in the empty streets. Sixty miles an hour under the stars, with a frozen wind that made him tremble like he did at the end of a week of drinking. José Daniel Fierro shoved his cap down over his brow with his free hand.

"Almost there, chief. In the Esmeraldas neighborhood. The one behind the hill on the main highway."

"Who lives there?"

"Ranchers, the mine owner, businessmen, Mercado's parents, the director of the middle school, the engineers of the Ag Department's experimental fields, the PRI ex-mayor, one of my sisters-in-law . . ."

"You can stop now."

They entered the highway and Barrientos accelerated even more. Then he took an open curve and José Daniel felt like his teeth would fall out when the frozen air hit his face.

The red car was at the end of a street. Alone. Lómax next to it on the bike. Blind Man braked noisily in front of Popocha's motorcycle, lifting the loose gravel. JD got down, rubbing his hands to bring them back to life.

"No more cars?"

"They keep them all in garages."

JD walked around the car while his boys watched. It was locked. Lómax lit up the inside with a flashlight. The keys were not there.

"One or the other, they abandoned it here without leaving a trail, or they didn't think we would find it so quickly and it has to do with someone who lives in those houses."

"That's it, now you've got it, because in that house lives the big cheese himself," said Blind Man, smiling.

"Which one?"

"Melchor Barrio, the PRI boss."

"Shall we pay a visit?"

"At five in the morning without speaking to Benjamín first? I don't think so."

"Lómax, find the patrol car, and tell them to bring Benjamín here, get him out of bed."

"Which bed?" asked Lómax. "Where's he sleeping tonight?"

"Who knows," said Barrientos.

"Shit," muttered José Daniel.

He walked around the red car again. He heard crickets, and an automatic hose watering the garden behind the stone walls of the house. A street of walls, castles shut off by fences from the rest of the city. Only two houses on one side, and one on the other, that of the PRI boss.

"There are armed men inside there," said Blind Man.

"So?"

"Just so you know, so you don't say I didn't tell you."

"Popochas, bring a tow truck and take the car to the jail patio. I believe that's all for today."

34.

Notes for the History of the Radical City Government of
Santa Ana
José Daniel Fierro

━━━━━━━━━━━━━━━━━━━━━━━━━━━━━━━━━━━

Since Benjamín and his gang came to power, crime in Santa
Ana has been transformed. Murders have increased, no doubt
a product of the heightening of social conflicts. Common
robbery has diminished, a product of who knows what. Official robbery has disappeared. Sex crimes have increased,
maybe the heightening of the class struggle makes some people crazy. Divorce has risen at an alarming rate (from 27 a
year to 103). The town's fortune-tellers (two) are receiving
fewer clients. Theft of cars, motorcycles, and bicycles has
practically disappeared. Street assaults are a thing of the past
(some of the gangs joined the movement, and the others,
according to Blind Man Barrientos, were given twenty-four
hours to clear out of town). Accusations of insult and injury
have multiplied by eight. Arrests for public drunkenness have
diminished. Arrests for traffic accidents have diminished.

Begging has disappeared. Public attention to venereal disease has almost disappeared. Arrests for offenses against public health have increased. One citizen was arrested for farting at the movies. Six bosses were arrested for not paying minimum wage. It is not hard to draw conclusions.

35.

Hotel Florida, Dawn

He left the shotgun behind the door. He walked to the small bathroom and verified there was no one inside. Then he stood before the window to watch the light stain the white walls of the main street. In his hands he carried the perforated and bloody yellow dress and a folder with the photos of the child. A six-year-old boy, blond like the dead woman: leaving a nameless school, in a city full of cars with California plates, eating an ice cream cone, smiling before the monkey cage, sleeping in a very small bed with white sheets, sucking his thumb.

José Daniel felt extremely old. He thought he could just as well pack his bags and walk to the bus station. It was a night as good as any other to say goodbye to Santa Ana.

He looked in the mirror. A doom-laden new mania for confirming that he was still on his feet with his baseball cap. Santa Ana was making him old. Or was simply making him a super-survivor at the edge of retirement. He vacillated be-

tween getting up to sing "Venceremos" or a Gardel tango
that spoke of gray hair, between falling asleep on his feet
like a horse or masturbating while thinking of Greta Garbo.
That was a symptom of old age. The whole world masturbates
thinking of Jane Fonda or Olga Breeskin, according to their
taste, while he still concentrated on ranchero singers wearing
wide skirts down to their ankles and cowboy hats.

Poor José Daniel Fierro, so much owner of his typewriter
and so out of his element. So much owner of other people's
dreams, so solitary in his own nightmares. So afraid of putting
a comma in the wrong place and so newly rich in wounds,
cadavers, human plunder, and terrors.

As always, Santa Ana's dawn got under his skin and re-
vived old droughts. He put out the electric light, in the tenuous
gloom his image in the mirror came undone and appeared
cadaverous. He shifted his cap a bit to the right and then
straightened it. If he hadn't wanted to, he wouldn't have
accepted. Now he had only to leave Santa Ana with a Guggen-
heim grant, heading into exile with a legion of failures (and
he with the last shotgun in hand); that, or go out walking
alongside the last ambulance without daring to look behind
so that his flaming boots would not turn into salt.

Now he had only to discover the murderers of the girl who
wanted to be Jessica Lange and in whose body they buried
a kitchen knife.

He sat on the bed and looked in the mirror again. He got
up again and walked to the door and picked up the shotgun.

He slept with his boots and cap on, lovingly cradling the
breech-loading shotgun.

Smiling.

36.

Confessions

⌁⌁⌁⌁⌁⌁⌁⌁⌁⌁⌁⌁⌁⌁⌁⌁⌁⌁⌁⌁⌁⌁⌁⌁

He opened one eye and got up on his elbows, frightened. There was someone in the room, the shotgun fell to the floor.

"No problem, chief, I put on the safety. What an ass you are with firearms, you slept with the safety off."

José Daniel Fierro scratched his head.

"And why are you here so early, Blind Man? What time is it?"

"Eight. You just got two and a half hours' sleep, chief," said Blind Man Barrientos, walking to the washbasin and taking off his glasses. He let the water run from the tap and began to carefully clean the mucus out of his eyes, making walrus noises at the cold water.

"What's new?"

"I went out fishing for rumors, chief, instead of sleeping."

"And how do you do that? You'll have to teach me."

"You go here and there, looking for the worst gossips,

you give them two words and get ten in return. It's easy. The only problem is that seven in the morning isn't the best hour for hunting down gossips—around here everyone's a bit fucked up at that hour.''

''Including the chief of police.''

''That's true . . . During the revolution, there was a Villista colonel who used to come here, Colonel Cabrera Palomec, and he only came for gossip, they told him what was happening hundreds of miles away. He said that nowhere did they speak of the revolution so prettily as in Santa Ana. Once he beat up the Federales in Las Tunas, forty-four miles to the north of here, and he came running to Santa Ana so we could tell him about the battle.''

José Daniel pushed gently at Blind Man, who was now using the chief's brush to comb his hair at the mirror, so he could wash his face too.

''And what's the gossip?''

''That this isn't the first time the gringa has come to this town . . . There's shit in the air, chief,'' finished Blind Man enigmatically.

JD stared at him. Blind Man tucked his shirt into his pants, carefully, hoping for a semi-martial air.

''Our hosts?''

''I sent Lómax and Merenciano to sleep. Martín, the Russian, is guarding the gringa's car; Greñas is out patrolling the town on the bike.''

''I'll walk to the office. Ask the owner of the bookstore to come by and see me right now.''

José Daniel left the Hotel Florida and was surprised at the force of the sun that stung his face and back. To buy dark glasses would be too expensive. Some middle school students, late for class, crossed his path. He felt their eyes at his back, but it was not the sullen look common to Mexicans when faced with the law, they were looks of solidarity. At first opportunity he would get a middle school pin to put next to Spiderman. The April 20 popular middle school was one of his favorite spectacles in Santa Ana. Hundreds of greensweatered adolescents walking on the edge of the highway in the middle of the afternoon.

The nine cups of coffee were still lined up on his desk. A brilliant light broke the office into stripes through the venetian blinds. He turned on the coffee pot after verifying there was water, and changed the coffee. Then he walked the few steps to the radio station. Fritz was at the controls; at his side, skinny Canales slept on a diminutive cot from which his legs protruded a foot.

"And we continue with our program to begin the day. For you, the *Clair de Lune*. Music to soothe the early morning here at Radio Santa Ana."

Fritz cued up the record, turned to JD, pointed at the sleeping Canales.

"Look at him, he's got me playing music for siestas. If he doesn't wake up soon, I'll play the Russian army chorus and then Beethoven's *Eroica*. And the other bastards go on interfering with our signal from the mountain."

"Did anyone call?"

"About the dead woman? A lady who has a taco stand on Calle Lerdo, Doña Luisa, half a block from the church. She wouldn't tell me shit even though I told her I had a right to the information. She wants you to go by. Two calls threatening death to Benjamín, saying that now he's in deep shit."

"Is that normal?"

"Every other day."

JD saluted, lifting a finger to his cap, and went back to his office.

Barrientos was serving two cups of coffee when he entered.

"Esther says she can't leave the store right now, she's expecting some cartons of books from Mexico City and you should go by there or wait another half hour . . . They reported a robbery in the Conasupo warehouse, I sent Greñas out there."

"Is the bookstore far?"

"Five blocks alongside the main street, on Revolución, toward the south."

"I'll walk to the bookstore and then go by the jail to see the car, and from there I've got to see a lady at a taco stand in front of the church. You take charge of the robbery and when the Russian appears send him to sleep when Lómax and Merenciano report in . . . It's all very heavy. Sleep a bit here. Steal the cot from our neighbors at the radio."

Barrientos agreed.

The bookstore was very narrow, with two long series of shelves down the sides with floor-to-ceiling books and some small tables in the middle that ended with a desk that served as a counter and the owner's office. JD tried to go directly to her but could not. One and a half yards from the entrance he stopped in front of a bookcase of Latin American literature when he saw Soriano's *There Will Be No More Pain or Forgetting*. A book he'd been looking for for years. Beside it, *The Compañeros* by Rolo Díez, just out, a novel they talked about in Mexico City, about the last years of the Argentine madness and the guerilla movement. He went on browsing, squatting before the bookshelves. He had forgotten why he was there.

"It's true it doesn't look like a small-town bookstore, does it?" said Esther.

"Not at all," answered JD, finding a book of Onetti's stories in the Contemporary Times edition that he had owned and been robbed of years ago. Son of a bitch! There were the first two novels of Iverna Codina and *Bolero* by Lisandro Otero in Cuban editions.

"You have to sign your novels, José Daniel, here in the detective section."

JD took his books and followed the woman to the fourth bookcase. There were seven of his novels, some in old editions no longer on the market. Also the new detective story by Orlando Ortiz and some old editions of Caimán and the Seventh Circle.

"Ouf," said Chief Fierro.

"I knew you'd like it. We have books here you can't find

anymore in Mexico City. I go out and buy things here and there. Look, I have something like fifteen books of the Maigret series by Simenon at five hundred pesos.''

JD looked at the bookstore owner with admiration. It was much better to read than be chief of police. It made the question that followed an act of masochism.

"The gringa who was killed was here yesterday?"

"Anne? They killed Anne? I thought you wanted to talk about books. Nobody told me anything.''

"Her name is Anne?" asked José Daniel, holding out some Polaroid photos. Esther stared at them.

"Poor sweetie.''

"Have you known her a long time?"

"She came last year, she was the photographer for a magazine in Los Angeles. We're folkloric, a radical town and all that. She came to the demonstrations. She bought some books here, underground novels of the 1960s that I have in the back, the sort of thing the local gringos like. She was nice, spoke Spanish. This time she came to buy some books, she said she couldn't sleep. She bought a pocket edition of *The Naked and the Dead* by Mailer and a biography of Bob Marley. We talked for ten minutes. She looked tense.''

"She didn't say who else she wanted to see? She didn't talk about Santa Ana?''

"She said she was going to take photos of the palm weaving cooperative at City Hall, and she wanted to see Benjamín, but she seemed to be thinking of something or somewhere else.''

"And the gringos?"

"Which ones?"

"The ones who live in Santa Ana.''

"They're a colony of some fifteen families, Vietnam veterans; almost all of them are retired with pensions for the disabled. With what they get, they live very well here. In Kansas City they would starve. They're nice, they keep their problems to themselves, they don't hang out much with natives like me. They all have something to do: a pottery kiln, one woman paints with watercolors, one studies German by correspondence and doesn't speak Spanish. They come here to buy books and place orders I fill through American Book in Monterrey. I never saw them with Anne.''

"Nobody knew her yesterday but you tell me she was here last year taking photos.''

"Just for a few days. I remembered her because one day we spent hours talking about photography books. She adored Robert Capa and Cartier-Bresson. She liked the same photographers as me.''

"And me.''

JD left the bookstore with forty-seven books and not a penny in his pocket. He had spent half his salary on books. He carried them in two packages tied with cord with the shotgun dangling from his back. It was a very strange war. He remembered the Capa photo of the dead parachutist and then immediately the posture of the woman in church. Were her cameras in the car? She too was a photographer.

The Russian showed him the open trunk, inside were the two cameras, a six-by-six Nikon and a Minolta with a wide-angle lens. The blue suitcase was there and the automobile registration with her data: Anne Goldin, 116 Riverview, San Jose, California, the books Esther had told him about, and a two-piece bathing suit, damp.

"Does anyone know how to take fingerprints?''

"Who knows, chief. I could ask Lorenzo, a friend in the PO who's a chemist for the University of Mexico.''

"The judicials know we have the car here?''

"They haven't come by.''

"Do we have police seals?''

"No. What's that?''

"Papers you tack on the doors with gum and a sign saying that the car is evidence and the seals can't be broken.''

"I'll do it, that's easy.''

"It won't work for shit,'' said José Daniel, just to be an

ass. "Take my books and the suitcase with the cameras to the office, then make the seals, come and stick them on, and go home to sleep."

"Tomás told me they robbed the Conasupo, can I go?"

JD looked at him strangely. Of all his agents, Martín Morales, alias the Russian, was the taciturn, silent one. He was surprised at the vehemence, the determination in his voice.

"My sister is a cashier there."

JD nodded. The Russian began to carry everything on the back of the motorcycle using string to tie the load. JD left the patio of the jail and tried to orient himself. The church was six blocks down Calle Lerdo, and Lerdo was at the next corner. He set off with a tired step. The sun shone on white walls, making the graffiti jump out. Lately the most common was a replica of the one the chief of police wore on his cap: SANTA ANA WILL WIN! Who conspired against the city by killing a blond North American, mother of a six-year-old child, and left her naked inside a church?

"There were two, chief," said Doña Luisa, but not before Chief Fierro had accepted a Corona Extra for the heat.

The woman pointed with her whole arm to the entrance to the church. JD nodded.

"I only saw them from afar, because I don't go in there. I'm Protestant, chief, and with the Popular Organization. But from far off I saw there were two guys who got into the car, one with a Stetson hat, the other in a suit. And I thought and I thought all night and I couldn't say anymore. I saw the car and half believed that that heretic priest, that bigmouthed asslicker of the rich, didn't have a car and much less a red one, it wouldn't stick, and I saw the two leave and start the car. Then I went to see my comadre who's sick and so I didn't know about the trouble till my daughter told me, and I spent the night thinking on how the two of them looked, but I barely saw them. One with a Stetson and the other in a navy blue suit."

"Who drove, Doña Luisa?"

"Let me see," the woman frowned as if reconstructing

the scene. "The one with the suit got in the driver's side because the one I saw better was the one with the hat."

"Would you recognize them?"

"Only if they're dressed the same, and you put them far away from me, or in other words I don't think so."

"I thank you very much."

"Get them, chief. Nobody should come to Santa Ana to kill nobody, even from the outside . . ."

"That's what I'm doing."

The woman took the empty beer bottle and gave José Daniel a kiss on the cheek. This disconcerted him. She was short and very fat and had to get on the tips of her toes to kiss him.

"It seems to me the priest is also a fag," she said, amplifying her information in farewell.

JD, who was of Jacobin background, nodded.

He entered the old black stone building surrounded by chattering secretaries returning from lunch. On the staircase the mayor, Benjamín Correa, waited for him, tense. He stopped in the middle of the stairs.

"They're going to try to stick me with the murder, chief," said Benjamín. "I was with her yesterday."

37.

Notes for the History of the Radical City Government of
Santa Ana
José Daniel Fierro

~~~~~~

When you try to put Santa Ana's tensions down on paper to
explain the radical government, its origins, the particular
convergence that permitted the union of forces that impelled
it, the weakness of the enemy that functioned like a stage
curtain for the convergence, one has to combine the study of
slow processes with rapid situations. Santa Ana, like anywhere else in the country, moves with a combination of tensions that come from the past, with the rapid succession of
small happenings that go on building into agitated waves.
Macario, the leader of the miners' union, tries to explain it
when he says that Santa Ana is a place where nothing happens
because everything happens. Nevertheless the city I'm getting
to know doesn't look like the one they tell me about. I feel
as if a backwater had been produced, a time of waiting, a
stage when small events accumulate to unfold into something.

As for Benjamín, if anything characterizes him it is an irrational sensibility of the social, he repeats to me every time he can: "Something is moving toward us and we still don't feel it, but it will be serious. They're very quiet." Not the product of conscious forces, or that's what he thinks, the government's enemies are waiting, or embarked on reorganization, in mythical operations that give no results, in moments of the great campaign of attrition, which is the only continuum one perceives here, or else they're preparing something big we don't know about. But there are other things, things in the air, responses to calls made a few years ago, illusions buried in the city, cold hearths that are warming. In the long run, Santa Ana is a pit in a country of injustices, there are debts two or three centuries' old, personal affronts that are historical and that originated one afternoon in April in the middle of the nineteenth century when the mine owner made the peons of shaft number two eat the flesh of a dog they had killed by accident.

In the short run, Benjamín's bearded ones have gone around to all the ranches to talk about irrigation and painfully organizing the campesinos of the seven municipalities around Santa Ana. In the short run there is a debate in every household with a child in the middle school over the workers' right to the factories where they work. In the short run there are tensions in the two small steelworks that are all that remain of the union booty of the CTM in the area. In the short run they speak of unionizing the maids, and say that two gunmen came from Mexico City to kill Benjamín.

In the long run there is the problem of the demarcation of the lands between the colonies of Cerro Viejo and Don Sabás, which remains unresolved only by grace of the old man's machine guns. In the short run there is the debate over how to make the old movie theater a cooperative, and in the long run the debate over whether we should preserve the language of the two hundred Chichimeca campesinos of the Cañada. In the short run Don Eligio, the priest of Santa Isabel, reads

liberation theology texts and in the long run the widows,
daughters of miners' widows, dream of blood.

I know that I must put things down on paper to avoid
surprises. Benjamín, who sees me taking notes, does not
believe in private paper, and together with Fritz has spent a
week designing a weekly wall newspaper.

38.

Nothing to Do

▲▲▲▲▲▲▲▲▲▲▲▲▲▲▲▲▲▲▲▲▲▲▲▲▲▲▲▲▲▲▲▲▲▲▲▲

The halls of the first floor of City Hall were occupied by the women of the straw hat weaving cooperative. Be it populist folklore or lack of space, Benjamín moves well among the women making the hats who fill up the space, many times up to the door to his office, joking and singing while they work. On the other hand, the representatives of the state and federal government feel like they're in enemy territory, watched over by witnesses who impede rule number one of Mexican political power: action in the shadows, the coverup. Benjamín's witnesses, symbolic representatives of Santa Ana, make City Hall into a kind of festive factory. The women, nearly all of them more than fifty years old (for this the factory was created, to give work to women who would not be given jobs in industry), have a curious attitude about Benjamín: they consider him a mixture of son and godfather, take care of his meals and pinch his butt when he goes by, bring him beer, and pretend not to notice when one of the secretaries spends more than half an hour alone in the office with its mayor.

José Daniel and Benjamín passed among them that morning, spattered with jokes and recently wetted straw. The office was curiously empty.

"I was with her yesterday afternoon," said Benjamín. "Women will be my ruin, José Daniel. They make me stupid. I met the little gringa last year when she was here shooting photos. Yesterday I ran into her in the street, she stopped her car and took me to the waterfalls, where we had a roll in the hay. But that's all, chief."

"What do you know about the child?"

"What child?"

"She had photos of a child. I believe a child of hers in California."

"First time I've heard. The truth is I don't know anything about her except her name was Anne and she was a photographer."

"Do you know if she had any other relations with the town?"

"I don't think so. Maybe with the gringo veterans, but the truth is I never saw her with them. That is, I never saw her. Last year two or three times when she took photos of the land seizure, and once when she took photos of me here in City Hall, and another time I found her in the bookstore and we had dinner together, but nothing more. She was a good person."

"Where were you going when you found her yesterday? What time was it?"

"Around five o'clock. I found her in Calle Revolución. Or rather she stopped her car and found me. I was coming from a meeting with the organizers of the La Libertad neighborhood, eating an ice cream, and she stopped behind me. A red car with California plates."

"What time did you leave her?"

"Don't you want a beer?"

"No."

"I left her . . . No, she left me here at City Hall, at the corner because the street is one-way, around nine o'clock, I had a cabinet meeting."

"Where were you at ten o'clock?"

"The meeting began around nine-fifteen; here are the minutes."

"They killed her at ten."

"Shit."

"So you have an alibi."

"For what it's worth . . . Who killed her?"

José Daniel shrugged his shoulders. Then he stretched out a hand for the offered beer.

"We found the car in front of the home of the PRI boss. Blind Man didn't dare go in to rouse them without consulting you first."

"The murderers took the car to that house or did they abandon it there?"

"I don't know. It all went very fast, it may be they were meaning to make it disappear."

"She took my photo at the waterfalls. There may be something else on that roll. Did you find the camera?"

JD nodded.

"We have a darkroom here in the offices of the PO, Sarita knows how to develop. Were they color or black and white?"

"Both."

"Chief, mount an attack on Melchor Barrio. If there's no proof, just tighten up. You have a free hand."

"And the judicials?"

"Them we have to stop in their tracks, so that they bite and don't fuck with the campesinos. No way, you'll have them on your back the whole way."

"You didn't have anything to do with the death of the gringa?"

"Nothing," said Benjamín looking him in the eye.

39.

Photos and Bribes

―――――――――――――――――――――――――

Radio Santa Ana had been alternating the militant songs of Joan Baez with the more militant tunes of Quilapayún. José Daniel intuited problems while he played at dusting his table with one finger. Before him, Blind Man Barrientos ate tacos of fried pork fat in green sauce with absolute parsimony, not letting a single drop drip on his trousers.

"Let him tell you. I have nothing to say."

"Don't hand me that shit, Blind Man. There's no such thing as two loyalties. You should have told me that Benjamín knew the gringa."

"Who knew her? Benjamín? Let him tell you."

"He already did."

"Okay, so that's that. You just got here. Benjamín and I have always been here, what the fuck are you saying?"

"You can't play if you don't know the game."

"He already told you, didn't he?"

JD nodded and drew hearts and sketches of little paper boats.

"When they kill someone, who are we committed to, respected Blind Man?"

Blind Man concentrated on the pork fat.

"To the dead, right?" asked José Daniel.

"Depending on who dies. If it's the chief of the judicials or a gunman sent from the capital, let his fucking mother watch over him, and let his fucking mother look for the killer."

"This was a little gringa of twenty-five with a six-year-old boy, who took photographs."

"Benjamín didn't kill her. Benjamín couldn't kill a woman. You want the guilty ones? Let's go look for them, don't keep fucking with me, chief."

"Okay, then, love and peace," said José Daniel Fierro. "What's happening with the photos?"

"They must be ready, I'll go and get them."

Blind Man left, trying to balance his pork fat tacos. JD got up and reviewed the contents of the suitcase for the third time; he skipped the clothing, opened the passport and leafed through it again; he preferred this photo of Anne to the Polaroid shots of the body. The girl had crossed the border on the 19th, her passport said she was married, but did not give her husband's name. JD noted the address in San Jose on a piece of paper so he could send a letter. Should the murder be reported to the consulate? He put the books aside. No papers, no letters. Nothing to look at. He lit a cigarette and walked to the door. Only the photos could tell him something.

"Reporting in," said Greñas in the doorway, with his hair over his eyes and his cheeks red, almost purple.

"What happened, Marcelo?"

"The Russian is getting first-aid, he'll be right here. And we left the two assailants in jail, also getting first-aid. So they're all in jail, three of them, getting first-aid."

"What happened?"

"We got scientific, chief. It was a little robbery, a little tiny fucking robbery. Two kids with a knife who emptied one cashbox, not even two. I was dealing with that and calming the cashier, who was really frightened because they scratched her throat to scare her, and the fucking Russian arrived all bent out of shape and asked her who they were. And after not saying a word to me, she told him immediately. We set out for the billiards hall on Calle Cinco, and there they were, two assholes shooting pool. The Russian gave them time to get out their knives and then fucked them both up. He left me watching the party. He bit one in the arm and took out a piece of flesh. That motherfucker won't get better, chief. But he stuck him a little bit. Here and here. Superficial, not submarine, just on top." Greñas pointed at his thigh and his hands. "They had the money on them."

"How's the Russian?"

"Good, chief, he'll be right here. He told me you shouldn't worry, he'll be right here, he's just putting a bandage on."

"And how did science enter into the matter?"

"The way the Russian beat up two of them at the same time. A fine thing."

"Greñas, if you had to choose between your hairdo and your job, which would it be?"

"Is this a game or do I have to cut my mop?"

"A game."

"No, then let somebody else decide. It really doesn't bother me when I'm riding the bike because I tie it back, look."

Greñas demonstrated his Apache drag while Blind Man came in with the photos and spread them out on the table.

"One roll was blank, the color roll; the other had only six photos; four of Benjamín, one of the filthy Priísta, and the other of the cripple who lives across the street."

"In the street where we found the car?"

"Exactly. A rich guy who's always in a wheelchair."

Blind Man pointed with his finger. They were professional photos, shot with a wide-angle lens from very close up, and captured the expressions well. Melchor Barrio, the PRI boss, complacent under a wide-brimmed hat, a cold and angular face, prematurely aged. The invalid, a man some thirty-five years old with very black hair and eyes hidden behind dark glasses, smiling from a wheelchair that a butler in a white jacket with wide shoulders and shining face pushed toward the door of his house.

"Which was first?"

"The one of the Priísta and the guy in a wheelchair. Then the ones of Benjamín. Look at the shadows in this one, it's noon," Barrientos pointed out.

"We're going to visit the bad guy of the film," said José Daniel. After hesitating an instant, Blind Man opened a drawer in the file cabinet and took out the square .45, twin of the one he carried on his belt, together with a box of bullets.

"We're not waiting for the Russian?" asked Greñas. "There's a dozen killers in that house."

"We're just paying a call," said JD smiling. "They don't do anything to visitors."

40.

Dear Ana/April 21

Dear Ana/April 21
    Fritz Glockner made some kind of lay scapulars out of wood, the kind you hang around your neck with a leather thong, and put that phrase that Pablo Milanes made so famous: "No one is going to die, least of all now" inside them and we gave them to the Santa Ana police force. I tell you this because if they lose, it will be your responsibility not to recommend it.

I love you. JD

41.

A Four That Comes out Eight

But Greñas lifted the phone, and after listening five seconds stopped them with his hand.

"Benjamín says not to go anywhere."

"And how does he know we're going out?" asked José Daniel. "Give me the phone."

JD took the phone, his head was beginning to hurt. "Chief of Police, sir, stop by here," said Benjamín, a little more opaque than usual.

"Blind Man, I leave you in charge of the office, take a break," he said as he hung up. He deposited the shotgun behind the door and pressed his temples with two fingers.

"Do you have any aspirin?"

"No, but I'll get you some . . . Lulú, aspirin for the chief!"

Benjamín was seated very formally at his mayoral desk. José Daniel had never seen him thus. Always dancing among people and furniture, always fleeing the formality of you sit here and I sit on the side of power. Always with a button missing from his shirt sleeve, always with a sauce stain on the collar of his jacket, always with a beer in hand when it shouldn't be; always watching the wrong side of the office, the window, the city, contemplating other things.

"They are waiting for you. Inside Barrio's gunmen, outside Durán Rocha's judicial police. They're going to fill you with lead and then mount a riot so they can ask the army to intervene."

"And how did they know we were going there?"

"They have ears here."

"How did you know they were waiting for us?"

"They're not the only ones with ears. I have an enormous ear of a hundred seventy thousand little ears; many of them don't appear as such. What does your baseball cap say? 'Santa Ana will win.' Do you think we would put that on every yellow cap we can find if we didn't even have a chance?"

"Here are your aspirin, chief," said the secretary. JD threw them into his mouth without breaking them and swallowed them without water.

"You have to show me how to do that."

"A trained windpipe. Do you think I could write eleven novels without learning any tricks?"

"The worst is that Barrio believes we are pulling a trick on him. That we want to charge him with the death of the gringa, that's why he's acting so fierce."

"You mean you think he had nothing to do with it."

"You should find out. He or the fifteen killers who live in his house, or his secretary who's an asshole, who when he was in government and thought he owned the city raped ten-year-old girls. You'll see. Or do you want us to believe that he's enraged and in the end the murders are his?"

"What do you suggest?"

"That you wait and later go by yourself, or with all the Mexico City journalists we can get together."

"Let me think about it."

"Let me know. Things are heating up here."

"Anything I should know?"

"The rumor is that they're cooking up something big for us. That's why they're so quiet."

"So?"

"We can't stop, because if we stop we'll die a natural death. Listen, do me a favor: we need to distract the judicials, tomorrow there will be a big land seizure out by La Cañada. Two thousand campesinos with their families and everything. They've been preparing for months. Haven't you heard the rumors? They were communal lands and eleven years ago the caciques took them at gunpoint. Now there's a rumor going around: *Tomorrow we'll come back, tomorrow we'll come back.*"

"You mean I have to entertain the judicials and think about how to get at Barrio?"

"That's it."

"You know the city, Benjamín; who killed the gringa?"

"I have no idea, José Daniel, no fucking idea."

In the hallway he found Martín Morales, the Russian, with bandaged hands. JD put his arm across his shoulders, paternally, and they entered the office together, in silence, JD imagining ten thousand campesinos pulling out posts and wire fences.

"So what now, chief?" asked Blind Man.

"They're waiting for us."

"Are we going?"

"Not till they've stopped waiting . . . Russian, go and tell them at the radio to announce that the dead gringa's car was found in the street where that gorilla lives and that the investigation continues."

The Russian left to fulfill his commission. JD fell into a creaking armchair. Greñas and Barrientos watched him, waiting.

"Greñas, to the street, normal patrol. The town has to see that we're still keeping on."

Greñas left without saying a word.

"Let's see, Blind Man, who lives in those three houses where we found the car? Who is that cripple? What are the houses like inside? You who know everything and invent what you don't know, stuff me with information."

"Barrio's house, the first one, is big, with a garden of some thirty yards in front. I've never been inside. He must have a dozen gunmen, with automatic weapons. No family. No one can stand him. He has a daughter but she left years ago, she's a nurse, she lives in Mexico City . . . In the second house the man in the wheelchair. He's a millionaire, his name is López, he had an accident about five years ago and came to hole up in Santa Ana. They say his family was from around here. He had never been in town before, he was a jet-setter, Rolls-Royce, house in the United States . . . He never goes out. Sometimes doctors come from Mexico City. He has the fag in the photo and a maid, that's all. The fairy pushes the wheelchair and cooks. I've never seen him armed or anything . . . In the third house, on this side, in front of where we found the car, lives the widow of the Chinaman Ling, who owned all the big businesses of Santa Ana. The widow has enough money to paper her walls with. She lives with her daughter, who's very hot shit and wants to be a rock singer. Sometimes you see the young Chinese with the gringos from the Estrella colony. She can't sing for shit, but she comes on good, with that she'll triumph, right?"

"With less than that in Televisa they'll make a six-chapter series with ranchero ambience."

"With a Chinese?"

"With half, Barrientos. I can see you haven't been out much."

"Less than I wanted to, chief . . . Do you really think it's in that street? Just because of the car?"

"It's that you can see everything two ways. Either they had the car parked there because they didn't think we'd find it so quickly . . . but then they would have taken the suitcase and the cameras . . . Or someone put it there to tell us something or to tell them something. It's like those messages that come and go. Even though they don't want to say anything, if you know who they're for, you learn something."

"And why don't we look somewhere else? For the guy with the Stetson hat and the one in the navy blue suit. Them and the car between nine and ten last night."

"And how do you know that?" asked José Daniel, very surprised.

"I spoke with the lady too, chief. Did she give you a beer?"

JD nodded.

"And two for me. Because I'm a native."

JD smiled. "Leave it at that, I believe you . . ."

The chief of police of Santa Ana stopped, hearing cries in the street. It sounded like waves. He looked out the window. A crowd of miners had congregated before the building, climbing the grillework of the church, raising their fists.

"Shaft number three is on a work stoppage, because of the uniforms . . . It's going to heat up," said Barrientos without looking outside.

JD was by now used to everyone knowing everything, except for him. "And what do we do now?"

"We have to put a guard at the entrance to the mine so the scabs don't enter and provoke fights."

In the street were some eight hundred miners whose slogans began to merge into one, "Santa Ana will win!"

"Chief, another one," said a red-faced Greñas, entering the office.

"Another what?"

"Another death." He let himself fall into the folding chair.

"Now what?"

"They found Blackie dead."

"The PRI gunman?"

"Exactly," said Blind Man. "Where?"

"In the circus, shot six times."

"Son of a bitch, are we going to see him first or shall we
celebrate right now?" asked the assistant chief of police of
Santa Ana with a smile that almost rattled his teeth.

42.

Notes for the History of the Radical City Government of
Santa Ana
José Daniel Fierro

━━━━━━━━━━━━━━━━━━━━━━━━━━━━━━━

Manuel Reyna, Blackie, has a dossier of some fifteen sheets
in the files of the municipal police of Santa Ana. The purpose
of the file is to preserve the town's history for the day of
justice. Justice arrived and no one knows how. That left a
strange taste in the mouth. The data now belongs to a cadaver
tossed in the middle of the circus ring.

I have read the history twice: a salesman of agricultural
machinery, albino, who got into heroin in the petroleum
camps of Campeche, beat a woman to death, was tattooed
with a plumed serpent on his left arm, and then appeared in
Santa Ana to do the dirty work of the state government.

The brains behind every provocation, spearhead in every
confrontation, he had (had had) a singular status, answering
neither to Barrio nor to Don Sabás, nor to any of the local
strongmen; he played ball with neither the judicials nor with

those sent by Mexico City, but answered only to the state government. He did not live in town, he was not a tough guy tied by blood and debts to the needs of the local political bosses. He was a gunman on salary, solitary, who sometimes appeared over Santa Ana like a bird of bad omen, always keeping his back covered, always both far and near, always alone and with a fixed target.

In the file were two photos of the day he fired upon the demonstration from the cathedral with a machine gun. Blurred photos, Stetson hat(!). Then incidental news of his travels while the collective assassination got cold in the pages of the Mexico City papers.

An appearance three months ago heading up a group of gunmen hired by Don Sabás to fire on the campesinos of La Piedad ranch. A typed report that accused him of having killed Lisandro Vera, the student and first chief of police of Santa Ana, with his bare hands after having tortured him.

An Instamatic photo that showed him leaving a hotel on González Ortega with two suitcases.

To this one would now add the photos of his cadaver.

43.

Watching the Trapeze

The circus had pitched its tents on the vacant lots alongside the highway access; two big tents and a dozen trucks with some mangy bears and zebras persecuted by flies.

In the sands of the central tent, surrounded by dwarfs and trapeze artists and constituting the after-dinner spectacle, Manuel Reyna, Blackie, was thrown down. Hunchbacked, his body giving the impression of furious activity despite its immobility, due to the .45 caliber bullets that had twisted him into knots, leaving him covered with entrance and exit wounds.

"Six shots, chief, all of them mortal, as they say."

"And his pistol, was it fired?"

"No, chief, they got him shitting. He must have got it out when he felt the first bullet, but didn't even have a chance to play with it," said Barrientos, who bit a toothpick between his teeth to keep from smiling.

"Are you happy, Barrientos?"

"I'm sorry it wasn't me who got him."

"Let's see! Don't move around too much . . . What is this? These are the boots of Greñas, and these are mine, look at the defect in the left heel. And those? Make a drawing of them. Surely they're the same as the bloodstains in the church. We need photos. Greñas, go get the teacher's Polaroid."

The best thing to do when faced with a corpse is to have no respect. So you can treat it like an object, without your heartbeat accelerating and your guts turning over. JD took his pulse. It was warm. Macabre cadaver of the albino. Unreal.

"What time was he found?"

"Here is the gentleman," said Greñas, taking the hand of a dwarf who quietly let himself be led to the writer.

"How did you find him?"

The dwarf put on his best circumstantial face to tell the story. "We waited till the shooting stopped and then picked straws to see who would come. There he was. Three-thirty in the afternoon, just a little while ago."

"Did you see him arrive?"

"It was dinnertime."

JD lifted his gaze to the immobile trapezes, the sky that peeked through the holes in the tent, then lowered it to the dead albino. Seen from afar he seemed to be smiling. As if saying, "Just look where I ended up."

"Barrientos, interrogate everyone, find out if they saw any cars at the entrance. Look at the tents. We are on open ground, the two guys arrived from somewhere, the dead man and the killer or killers. This one came from González Ortega as far as we know, he got here somehow. Look for the shells, here's one, there should be six. Take his boots off. Take his pistol and put it in a bag and bring it to the office. I'll be there."

44.

The Scent of Seven Machos

~~~~~~

One of the few Mexican contributions to the world of scents and perfumes is the cologne Seven Machos. Used in thousands of third-rate barber shops, it has an indescribable odor of overripe violets and cane alcohol. This is what José Daniel Fierro put on after shaving, and with two stiffs in the closet and only two and half hours' sleep on his bones, he went out walking in Santa Ana unarmed and without his cap. The absence of the gun was a matter of comfort; that of the cap, the vague impression that to wear it too much on sunny days would make him bald.

He left the door of the Hotel Florida and headed off to the right. The sun shone even at five in the afternoon, burning the asphalt and drying the few puddles left by the fruit vendors' melting ice. He advanced down Calle Revolución looking in the windows of the Chinese shopkeepers and the shoestores of Guanajuato industrialists who had come with their new boots to colonize the north of the country at the beginning of the 1980s. Once in a while he passed a traditional hardware store owned by a Spaniard with a name like Casa Toledo or Los Fierros de Oviedo, then two bakeries, a repair shop for agricultural machinery, a seed warehouse, a uniform shop. Arriving at the Cine Río, where they were showing *Nocaut,* he stopped to wait for the judicial who was following him.

"Do you have a moment, writer?" asked Durán Rocha.

"If the chat takes place in front of witnesses, I have no problem," said JD, smiling and at the same time feeling his asshole pucker up a bit. The chief of the judicial police based in Santa Ana awakened his deepest infantile terrors: with a tic that distorted his upper lip; a scarred face lost forever to any form of human encounter, forever calculating although there was nothing to calculate; with cold eyes that had spent thirty years burning in hell, Durán Rocha inspired panic in him. But JD had learned to transform his fears into words typed on a typewriter, and overcame his first impression.

"Right here, in the park."

They walked on, looking for shade under the laurels and a bench. They sat at a distance, leaving the center of the bench free, an uninhabitable space, a no-man's-land between them.

"You have nothing to do with this," Durán Rocha began. "This little game will be over one of these days and you will leave as if you'd never been here. Neither coming nor going. Santa Ana is not your concern. Your concerns are the letters defending human rights and the demonstrations in support of Nicaragua in Mexico City, cocktails at the Yugoslav embassy . . ."

"I've never been to the Yugoslav embassy, now that you mention it."

". . . and other such bullshit."

They were silent for a moment.

"The gringa and Blackie don't mean shit to me. There is already so much fucking death in this town that two more don't even give me insomnia at siesta time. I don't give a fuck who did it, it may be I did it and didn't notice. Or one of you, to heat things up. I don't give a shit. What I do want is for you to stop setting the journalists on my ass, because if you do it again, I'll kill you. You and all those fucking crippled assholes of the municipal cops. I'll make mincemeat out of you.''

''You know what the big difference is, Durán? It's that they're going to kill you in cold blood. Nameless women will drag your cadaver through the streets, spitting on you. You won't even be buried. But if you kill me, you'll have more journalists here than ever before, and they'll give me a funeral that will keep you awake nights. What do you think?''

''Once we're dead it's all the same. If the buzzards shit on me or if they put flowers on your dick, I don't give a fuck.''

José Daniel meditated on this response. The nearby benches were filling up with spectators. That was the curse of Santa Ana: you had to hide your fear and play to the audience. It was worse than in Hollywood; one put one's face on display for everyone.

''Who killed them, Durán?''

''I already told you I don't give a shit. I kill with a telegram in hand and there was no telegram for those two. Get out of this fucking town or you and I will not get old together.''

José Daniel got up and looked down at the man sweating in a dark suit. He couldn't tell him that he was already aged by their chat. He turned on his heel and left the chief of the judicial police talking to himself before the rapt looks of the spectators, and left behind him the potent odor of Seven Machos.

45.

Are You Writing a Novel?

~~~~~~

"We have seven reporters from Mexico City, two from Monterrey, and even one from *El Sol de San Luis Potosí*."

"Send them to the chief of the judicials, and then to Barrio's, tell them the car appeared in front of his house. And then tell them we'll have the pleasure of speaking with them at seven-thirty."

"Can they take a photo of me with the red car, chief?" asked Lómax.

"Whatever they like, my son," responded José Daniel Fierro, paternally. He was dying from lack of sleep.

"The guys at the radio want you to go by and see them for a minute. And Benjamín is waiting for you in his office when you're free," said the Russian.

"How are your hands?"

"Better."

"Tell them both I'm coming."

He remained alone in the room with Blind Man Barrientos.

JD lit his tenth cigarette. He was beginning to like the prole-tarian Delicados.

"What do you think?"

"You first. You're smarter in these things," replied Blind Man.

"There's something that doesn't fit and then many things that even though they don't fit are from the same puzzle. The guys who fired at me in the lunchroom. Do you know anything about that? Who they were? Who they could be?"

"I think they were Blackie's people. If you want I'll go looking in that direction. Shit, so much has happened in just a few days. Now all I need to do is get married."

"And do you have someone to marry?"

"Two," said Barrientos, smiling. "If I don't get married it's because I can't decide for the life of me . . . They look alike. They even have the same name: María, both of them, one just María and the other María Elena . . . But I wish all this noise would die down before I get married, I don't want to leave a widow."

Barrientos was seated on the file cabinet and smoking too, throwing his ashes behind him. José Daniel would have liked to have a tape recorder and make the whole story into a novel, two novels, three novels.

"I keep wondering why the car should have stayed on that street. It pushes me toward Barrio, toward the lame million-aire and the Chinese widow. It gets to me. It's too easy."

"That's probably why they put it there."

"Do you know something I don't know?"

"I know how to shoot."

"And aside from that?"

Blind Man Barrientos shook his head.

"I'll be right back. I'm going to see Benjamín and then to the radio station."

JD left the office, went through the halls and climbed the stairs with a dancer's tread. He went into Benjamín's office without meeting anyone. Around a small round table, bottles of beer in front of them, were the mayor, the lawyer Mercado,

Macario, the leader of the miners, two other miners he didn't know, and a campesino who looked very young.

"Am I interrupting?"

"Not at all, chief, we're talking about you and your murders," said Mercado.

"Anything new?" asked JD, pulling a chair up to the space they made for him at the table.

"In *El Heraldo* of the capital they say that the gringa was Benjamín's lover and that he killed her," said Mercado, laughing.

"I spoke with the governor's secretary and he said very nicely that if we push the people against Barrio and cause a riot they will fill the town with soldiers, but he said it as if they would do it anyway."

"That shit is always political," said Macario. "What if it was a crazy person?"

"What if it *was* a crazy person," repeated José Daniel, taken by the thought. "Or two crazy people, one for each crime. Or one of one and the other of others. Didn't we want to kill the albino?"

"It was vile justice, but if I had done it, or Blind Man, or Macario here, we would have taken him in González Ortega, or in Mexico City when he went for morphine at Barrio's daughter's sanatorium."

"The nurse?"

"What fucking nurse? She's the owner of a sanatorium in Las Lomas and she trafficks in drugs with medical prescriptions . . . Fucking rich bitch. Didn't you see the scars on the dead guy's hand?"

"New ones?"

"Old ones, on the right hand. Barrio has some too. They sat at the table in front of each other. They didn't like each other at all, but they used each other. They put a bottle of tequila in the middle and each one lit a cigarette, and then they took turns burning each other's hands, first Barrio to Blackie, then Blackie to Barrio, and the one who stopped smiling was the loser. Fucking pair of jerkoffs."

"Chief, whatever we tell you, you won't know the half of it. There are more than one hundred women in Santa Ana who have the same scars on their hands, from the days when that son of a whore was mayor. Blackie killed Valentín's brother and cut off his balls, and then went and threw them in front of his family's house," said Mercado, pointing to the young campesino. He got up and walked, stumbling a bit, to a bucket full of bottles of beer.

"We're all getting a little bit crazy from all the shit that's come down," said Macario.

"What should I do?" asked José Daniel, suddenly trapped in the vortex of Santa Ana's underworld, tossed by emotions and memories, watching Valentín's knuckles get white around the bottle of beer.

"This is a case for the police. Not to make any grand claims for the Santa Ana force, but before the inefficiency of the judicials, who dedicate themselves only to persecute campesinos and take care of the marijuana dealers so they can get their cut, we must take charge of the investigation. This is the official story and the real one for once. Here no one asks for anything to be covered up. Only for us to act together, because if we fuck up they will bring in tanks and chariots on parade and the most beautiful flowers of the army."

"To say nothing of their pricks," said one of the miners sagely.

"That goes without saying."

"You could have warned me when you brought me here," said JD.

"If we had known we probably would have stayed with you," said Macario.

"No, about the rain, that it doesn't rain," finished JD and left without hearing their laughter.

Another seven halls, another twelve steps. Canales was waiting for him, smoking in the doorway of Radio Santa Ana.

"That asshole Fritz says nobody can smoke in the control room. He's nuts, that guy."

"Let's give him a Veracruz cigar to see if he can resist," said JD, and entered the cabin with the cigar held out in front.

Fritz saw it in the corner of his eye while he was speaking lovingly into the microphone. JD had noticed this before. This amorous relationship, broadcaster/microphone, almost masturbatory, the way professionals took it and caressed it, spoke to *it*.

"Songs for lovers at dusk in the voice of Angélica María of the 1970s, when to be in love was a challenge to destiny. Songs for lovers who are tired and nostalgic, or for irresponsible youth who don't buy their toothpaste in the Campos pharmacy, sponsor of this program . . ."

Fritz let go of the console switch and started the turntable, giving the lever a shove with his elbow. Professional skill.

"Thanks, man," he said, appropriating the cigar and lighting it without further ado.

"We wanted you to tell us how things are going," said Canales to José Daniel but looking at Fritz with murderous fury.

"There's not much to say. Everything is still very nebulous."

"As they say, the novel is at the stage of investigation. When there are so many false leads you don't know where you're going."

"The truth is that in mine everything is pretty clear. I'm going to give a press conference and when I arrange my thoughts to speak with the journalists I'll come and give you the news."

In the middle of the hallway Barrientos was fending off journalists, an ill-tempered look on his face.

"Good evening, colleagues." A pair of flashbulbs went off.

"What do you think of this affair? Not exactly a novel, is it, José Daniel?" said the correspondent of *La Jornada*.

"Do the two murders have anything in common?" asked the one from *El Sol de San Luis Potosí*.

"The commander of the judicial police says that you are an intellectual from the capital who never saw a dead person before. That it was irresponsible of the government to have named you chief of police, and of you to have accepted," said the one from *El Porvenir* in a northern accent.

"Have they identified the dead gringa? Why was she killed in church? Why did they kill that gunman at the circus?"

"Have there been crimes like this here before?"

"Are you going to write a book about all this?"

"Do you know how many killers there were?"

"When are you going to resign?"

"It is true that you have a shotgun and don't know how to take off the safety?"

"How many cops are on the force?"

"Aren't the crimes out of your jurisdiction?"

"How old are you, José Daniel?"

"Are you writing a novel?"

"Are you writing another novel?"

"Are you writing a novel about all this?"

46.

Dear Ana/April 21 (II)

⌃⌃⌃⌃⌃⌃⌃⌃⌃⌃⌃⌃⌃⌃⌃⌃⌃⌃⌃⌃⌃⌃⌃⌃

Dear Ana/April 21

Me again, but this time not to ask for anything (you could certainly send me the green stapler, though), but to send you a draft of a novel—keep it, it may be that one day I'll write it.

It is a novel of some very fucked-up crimes, but the important thing is not the crimes, but (as in every Mexican crime novel) the context. Here one rarely asks oneself who done it, because the killer is not the one who wants the death. There is a distance between the executioner and the one who gives the orders. The important thing is usually the why.

And so I think this is the story of various whys. The characters are not, as my neighbors at the radio station would say, very lucid; they are more opaque.

There is a touch of exoticism: an American, but she always appears out of place, accidental, caught in a story that is not hers.

There are other characters who are more sordid, more common. It is not the first time they have been involved in a crime, more likely it is the millionth time. Saint-Exupéry would identify them by their hearts, Lombroso by their looks.

They follow the very Mexican trade of hired killer.

I would like to work with that, but I can't identify with those characters, I don't know if their hands sweat or if their eyes water when they exercise.

In this novel they stink, because they dirty the landscape of a city in which there are neither beggars nor rain.

Two hundred pages of the novel must be dedicated to the absence of beggars and to tell how the cacti flower on the slopes of the mountain range; a good chunk to tell of the days of rain. The rest, only the rest, could be dedicated to these grim characters who spoil the landscape. What do you think?

I love you. JD

47.

The Smell of Marijuana

~~~~~~

He had asked the switchboard to put in a call to Marc Cooper in Los Angeles, an old friend who was a journalist, with whom he had once written the screenplay to a movie, and was stretching himself in the armchair that creaked as much as his joints when the call came through. He spoke with Marc for five minutes at the city's expense, mixing Spanish and English as the words halted or flowed over the telephone line. He was hesitating between a brandy or a coffee when Merenciano appeared: shining, recently bathed, with his hair plastered to his skull.

"Now go to sleep, chief, I'll leave you the patrol car and pick it up later at the door to your hotel. Leave the keys at the desk."

"You'll let me know if something happens?"

"I should let you know if something happens?"

"Exactly, and tell Blind Man to go and sleep, that we'll

see each other tomorrow morning and he can tell me . . . If you have a chance, find out all you can about the Chinaman and his widow, Mrs. Ling. Do that for me.''

''Mrs. Ling?''

''Exactly.''

At the hotel desk they gave him a message before giving him the key:

''There is a gentleman waiting for you in the bar.''

He was bald with a gray moustache, with good healthy color, dressed in a black leather jacket and gloves. He looked almost like a paternal and televisable bank official. Too bad about the troubled look and watery eyes.

''You don't know me, I am Sabás, but surely you have heard of me,'' he said, offering his hand. ''I sent you a gift when you arrived and you returned it. Very bad manners.''

The bar was empty, with a bored waiter and a television that nobody was listening to. Don Sabás had a bottle of cognac and two glasses in front of him. José Daniel served himself a double (or a triple, depending on the measure) and sat back stretching his legs and leaving the shotgun leaning on the table between them.

''I came to ask you a favor.'' Don Sabás spoke very slowly, relishing the vowels, as if his companion was slow to understand. ''Because you are not from around here, I do not know what you have heard about me; and as we haven't had the pleasure of meeting, I wanted to come and chat with you in person, without onlookers or intermediaries or messengers. I came to tell you that the affair has nothing to do with me. The two murders have nothing to do with me.''

''And how am I supposed to know that?'' asked José Daniel.

''Because if they were mine I wouldn't come to tell you anything.''

''And what are you going to tell me?''

''Things.''

"Okay, then tell me."

"I don't know if I should . . ."

JD got up, tossed down the rest of his cognac, and picked up the shotgun.

"When you want to tell me, give me a call. I'm too tired for this today."

"Sit down, don't be so impatient. Just think, you've been in such a hurry you haven't learned some of the things you should know."

"Like what?" asked José Daniel without sitting down.

"Like that the mine is stealing silver. They don't declare a third of what they extract. They are robbing the country. Silver goes from here to the border as contraband."

"I have two corpses, and you say they're not yours. I've been in Santa Ana for one week and the only thing I know is that I don't know why they would be yours, and so, with you here telling me they are not yours, the first thing I think is that they are. I don't know you even by hearsay, and the only thing they tell me is that the hundred and fifty-three kilos of marijuana that we captured the other day were your property, and not for you to smoke by yourself. Now you tell me some bullshit about the mine, and next you'll read me the program for the circus tomorrow . . . Either tell me who's responsible for two murders or we'll each go home to bed."

"Son of a bitch, but you're impatient."

"To be patient one needs eight hours' sleep."

"The gringa was killed by two guys, okay? One you already know, the other was Durán Rocha, head of the judicials."

JD sat down and served himself another double/triple cognac.

"Why?"

"Why else? Because they were paid to do it."

"By who?"

"That would cost more."

"How much more?"

"To forget about my ranches from now till the end of the year."

"Good night," said José Daniel and this time he did not even look back after saying goodbye.

48.

Land

A tense voice on the loudspeakers of Radio Santa Ana woke him up:

"Compañeros, they are invading the estates of La Cañada. The campesinos of San Carlos and Los Horizontes are taking back the land of La Cañada. Everyone to La Cañada to support them and offer solidarity with them . . . Attention, people of Santa Ana, the campesinos of Los Horizontes are taking back the estates of La Cañada . . ."

The town bells were ringing. José Daniel got up and put his face under the tap, letting the cold water run. At the door of the hotel Blind Man was at the wheel of the patrol car.

"I thought you might want to go."

JD threw his shotgun in the back seat and straightened his baseball cap in the rear-view mirror. His kidneys hurt. An old sign of fear.

"Is this inside or outside the municipality?"

"Outside, in the neighboring municipality, San Sebastián."

"So we're there as observers."

"No, in solidarity," said Blind Man, starting the car.

The secondary highway was full of people walking the shoulders on both sides, some with banners and signs. Many striking miners from shaft number three, all the students of the secondary school in their green sweaters, the market women, even the three trucks from the Coca-Cola plant where the unionized prostitutes traveled with red banners instead of bottles.

The police car advanced through the middle of the crowd, among sporadic applause.

"The takeover was at dawn. Everything quiet until now, is what they tell me," commented Blind Man.

"Yesterday I was thinking I don't know how to fire the fucking shotgun," said José Daniel.

"When we go back we can stop around here and I'll teach you."

"Were the boot prints the same?"

"They were different, but we don't know which prints to match with which boot."

"Blackie with the blood print in the church. That's easy."

Blind Man looked at him with a mixture of suspicion and admiration.

"You want more? The print of the boot in the circus will fit the boots of the chief of the judicials."

"Son of a bitch, you're not going to put me in the shade," responded Blind Man. "The guy who fired on us in the lunchroom, the one who ran out, is in González Ortega, hiding in a hotel and shitting with fear."

"And what does he do there?"

"He's waiting for something. And I was right, he was one of Blackie's men. Only now he's left without a boss."

The crowd went off to one side of the highway where you could see torn-down fencing. Behind them, on a small peak, a red flag.

"Shall we visit?"

They saw small fires. The invaders were eating breakfast. José Daniel thought that he would sell his kingdom for some frijoles charros.

49.

Raining in Santa Ana

It was raining in Santa Ana when they returned. The city had changed into a phantom collection of little streets whipped by sheets of water that veered from one side to the other of the avenue tossed by wind as if from buckets. The streets appeared narrower and José Daniel realized that the city was sloped and descended to its center; he saw the little rivers of water that poured down the sides of Calle Revolución toward the plaza.

"Do you like the rain?"

"Very much," replied the chief of police. "Do you?"

"It makes me sad," said Blind Man Barrientos. He drove in silence and stopped the car before City Hall. They got out trying to protect themselves under the eaves of the first-floor balconies.

The first sign of alarm hit when they reached the second landing and saw the crowds of people.

"Something in the office?" asked Blind Man and they

both ran. The thickest crowd was in front of the door to Radio Santa Ana. José Daniel and Blind Man made their way through. Desolate, Canales and Fritz were contemplating the broadcaster's chair, which they normally shared. A tape spun, whipping its tail. There was a man in the control chair with his back to the door. Blind Man, faster than the chief of police, spun the chair around. The body of Durán Rocha, chief of the judicial police in Santa Ana, stared at them, a third eye some inches from his nose crusted with dry blood and burned flesh. *The vultures have accompanied him*, thought JD.

"Let's go, kid," said Fritz. Canales came over to the microphones and changed the switch. Fritz stopped the tape and passed him the mike.

"We lament the temporary suspension of our transmissions, but we are here in the studio of Radio Santa Ana with Chief of Police Fierro and Assistant Chief Barrientos, performing the preliminary investigation of a crime." The voice of Canales, which trembled at the start, was gaining confidence. "Live from our studio, where someone put a dead man while those in charge of Radio Santa Ana went out to eat . . ."

"There's no blood, he was killed somewhere else," said Barrientos.

"That's true."

"Chief Fierro and Assistant Chief Barrientos comment that the cadaver is the man in charge of the judicial police here in Santa Ana, the famous and little-loved Durán Rocha, and also comment that the assassination was not committed here, as there are no signs of blood. The dead man is found in the chair that your servants normally occupy, so that we will have to change the chair in the future. He has a hole in his forehead . . ."

"A small caliber bullet, a .22, fired close up."

"He's cold," said JD.

". . . And was killed hours ago, because as you've been able to hear, the body is cold."

"Is there anyone in our office?"

"Do you need anything, chief?" asked Juan Carlos Canales solicitously. José Daniel couldn't help smiling.

"Please tell the members of the police force to report here along with someone with a Polaroid camera. Shit, let's see if we can take up a collection and buy one. And a doctor."

"You've already heard, esteemed radio listeners of Santa Ana. Chief Fierro needs his crew, a doctor, and a Polaroid camera, as a gift if possible . . ."

"Blind Man, take prints of his boots."

Fritz touched his arm.

"Benjamín is calling on the intercom."

JD took the apparatus.

"Three judicials are on their way. Avoid trouble. Negotiate. We don't want any gunfire or trouble. If you want I'll come down and lend a hand."

"I'll take care of it," replied JD and then said in Barrientos's ear: "Blind Man, search him and keep everything in a bag. The traitors are on their way."

Blind Man cocked his .45 without taking it out of its holster, and then went looking through the dead cop's pockets, putting the papers he found into a can for recording tape.

A small commotion at the entrance announced the arrival of the three judicials. The one leading them was wild-eyed, pistol in hand, shoving with his elbows.

"And now we have here with us three abusive members of the dead man's police force who are elbowing the onlookers crowding into the door of our studio."

"What the hell is going on here? Who killed the chief?" said the man.

"We know as much as you do. They put him here at dinnertime, when no one was here."

"We'll take charge of the investigation," said the man pushing JD. Suddenly he bent over. Blind Man had taken advantage of the crowd of people to shove the barrel of a .45 in his kidneys.

"You are listening to . . ."

"Just don't push."

"There's a doctor and a photographer on their way."

"No way, we're taking him. So, the crime didn't take place here?" said a second judicial, struggling to get through.

JD pointed to the chair.

"Look, no signs of blood. He's cold. They put him here. Someone wants to confront us."

"Son of a bitch, you are now confronted. If I see you . . ." said the judicial in a louder voice.

"Show some respect, asshole," said Blind Man, shoving the barrel a bit more.

"We are not responsible before the Radio Commission for the bad language emitted in this transmission live from the studios of Radio Santa Ana . . ." said Canales, now truly relishing the affair.

50.

Notes for the History of the Radical City Government of
Santa Ana
José Daniel Fierro

▲▲▲▲▲▲▲▲▲▲▲▲▲▲▲▲▲▲▲▲▲▲▲▲▲▲▲▲▲▲▲▲

Santa Ana was founded by a man who wanted to die and not
leave shit behind him. One Hernán Villalar, who had gotten
lost on the silver trails on the way from Zacatecas, who
carried a Chichimeca arrow in his back that he couldn't get
out and that was poisoning his blood. He stayed here because
he found two runaway Negroes named Simón and Sebastián
who hunted birds with slingshots and gave him bird soup to
eat. The fact that this happened in the middle of the seven-
teenth century does not prevent the official story from having
always been played essentially as the adventures of disillu-
sioned men, with no love of life, who founded great wealth
without meaning to.

And so the second character in the history of Santa Ana
is one of the Salinas family, Frenchified landowners who
robbed land from the communities, the land of Indians re-

leased from the mines, taking advantage of 19th century land reforms. A Salinas who answered to the literary name of Edmundo, and who committed suicide twice, the first time in Santa Ana with poisoned port wine and the second time in Barcelona when it occurred to the imbecile to challenge a pimp from Seville to a duel, and with that he entered the Pearly Gates.

Santa Ana has had a pianist of moderate fame, and a pair of bucolic poets who achieved distinction in the days of Porfirio Díaz. The three died of tuberculosis, colluding in the creation of the necrophiliac phantom that feeds on the traditional history of the city.

The phantom is nourished by the doings of an Englishman, general manager of the mines, who suffered from chronic boredom, and who collected sexual perversions, albums of photos and paintings of nudes by folk artists. They cut his throat, fortunately in Torreón, while he was taking a Christian boy whose cousin was expert with a razor.

After 1923, the story of the bad-blooded aristocracy was transformed into that of well-fed caciques, beginning with an Obregonista colonel named Salustio, maternal grandfather of Barrio. With him the dross of the postrevolution made its day, building on the stories of others, those who filled the ravines with wheat and excavated the tin to fill the dozens of thousands of wagons, and partook, why not, of the legendary suicides and tuberculars.

The colonel had a niece who threw herself from the church belfry after abusing cough syrup and believing she could fly. But this is a minor story, and the tradition is disappearing.

Since 1972, the Popular Organization entered the chronicle, the chroniclers changed, the big collective characters showed their teeth, threw flowers, and drank beer.

51.

New Science

He waited for Popochas/Lómax to count his money and took his place before the cashier. The Santa Ana police were paid at the end of the first and third week of the month (that is, around the 7th and 22nd of each month) and JD was paid his first complete month (a bonus for the shooting, Benjamín had said). After receiving the envelope he stepped aside to let Barrientos take his place before the cash drawer and he started counting the notes.

"Do they make mistakes sometimes, Popochas?"

"No, but it gives me great pleasure to count them."

Instead of going up to his office JD walked to the gate at the entrance to watch the rain. *What a shitstorm*, he thought, while the wind occasionally tossed water in his face.

"You have a call from the United States in the office, chief!" shouted Popochas from the first floor. JD went up running. Barrientos held the phone with one hand and a pen and piece of paper in the other.

"Marc! What do you know?"

His friend's voice, half in English and half in Spanish, began to unfold a story from nine hundred miles away.

JD noted on his paper: *single mother*, *without husband*.

He drew a butterfly. *Child with grandparents. Grandfather says child's father is Mexican. Friend's darkroom: strange stories father child. She never spoke. Mexico City seven years ago*. He drew a second butterfly.

"Are they coming for the body? You're coming? The *L.A. Times* will pay you? Next week? Yes, of course . . . Bring aspirin . . . A hug, old man."

He hung up and gazed at the paper.

"The Traitor had a bank account," said Barrientos, putting a checkbook on the table. "It says here he made a deposit of a million pesos yesterday," he said, showing the bank receipt.

"Anything else in his papers?"

"A letter from a whore in Juárez asking for money for her child."

"Everyone has children scattered around up there."

"Where are we going, chief? To González Ortega to look for Blackie's helper? To the street where we found the car, to talk to the three neighbors? To walk around town and be seen?"

"What about the boot print?" asked José Daniel.

"What do you know, it's the same."

"Popochas, get out the chalkboard."

"Are we going to have a science class, chief?"

"We're going to put things in order."

José Daniel looked out the window. The rain was stopping. The town outside the window was still the same Santa Ana, but he was not the same innocent stranger of the first days. Was it the rain? or so many things in so little time? The rain, he decided.

"Let's see. If this were a novel we would not need science—it would be clear as day that the Chinese widow hired the judicial cop and Blackie to kill the gringa, and then the cop killed Blackie and the Chinese killed the cop. Since it is not a novel, let's put what we do know on this side:

"Between nine and ten at night on April 20, they killed Anne Goldin with a kitchen knife in the church of Carmen. Two men: one we know by his boot prints is chief of the judicials, Durán Rocha, and the other, who was wearing a Stetson hat, could be Blackie . . ."

"What should I put on the chalkboard?"

"April 20, Anne/knife/nine to ten/Durán Rocha and Blackie, that last with a question mark at the end . . . Exactly. What questions shall we ask, Assistant Chief Blind Man?"

"How much does a bottle of Bacardi cost if the price of sugarcane in Veracruz has gone up seventeen percent in the last year and the vampire on the label is more cross-eyed than ever?"

"Where do I put that?" asked Popochas.

"Nowhere. All right, Blind Man, leave literature for Canales's garret. Questions?"

"Why? Why in the church and naked? Who paid?"

"Okay, put under Durán Rocha the million pesos that we know he had in the bank . . . How did those two get along?"

"Not very well. Gypsies don't read each other's hands. But it was competition. Durán Rocha had more friends among the town Priístas, he hung out more with them. Blackie was solitary. He came and went. For example, I never saw the two together."

"Neither did I," said Popochas.

"Neither did I, chief," said Greñas, joining the group of scientists.

"Okay, we'll go for the second round: the red car. The killers took it. It appears an hour and forty-five minutes later in a street where there are three houses."

"What do I write?"

"Red car. Street . . . What is the name of that street?"

"La Escondida."

"So. Then three houses: Widow Ling, Barrio, what is the cripple's name?"

"López, Engineer López."

"Okay. Greñas, why did the car appear there?"

"The murderers put it there to get something, to make a point."

"And why didn't they? The suitcase was inside. Why abandon it there?" It was becoming an inquiry, Maigret-style, but with too many questions.

"To confront Barrio," said Blind Man.

"They left the car in front to pressure one of the owners of the three houses. To increase the pressure to get more money. That's why the car was there. They left it there as a calling card," said JD, proudly.

"I like it," said Blind Man.

"Let's see, they paid those two bastards to kill Anne," said JD, nearly spoiling everything by using her name. Anne suddenly reappeared, a twenty-five-year-old California girl with a six-year-old son, not material to make "science" out of.

"Coffee, chief?" said Barrientos, guessing that something was going on. Merenciano entered the office in silence and took a chair, behind him, the Russian. The Santa Ana forces were complete.

JD nodded.

"So, after killing her they take the car and leave it in front of the house of the one who ordered her killed, as a reminder that he owed them something. What do you think?"

"Weren't they taking a risk?"

"We worked very quickly that night, didn't we."

"I guess so," said JD, feeling that after all the clarification nothing was particularly clear. "Third, we know that the judicial killed Blackie at the circus. Six shots from a .45 . . . What pistol did he carry?"

"A .45, like two thousand other inhabitants of Santa Ana, like me," said Blind Man.

"And fourth," continued JD without stopping, "whoever killed him ordered the murders."

"Why in the circus?"

"How the fuck would I know?" replied José Daniel.

"Really," said the Russian. "And why at the radio station?"

"In the church, in a circus, in the radio station . . . It seems to me they want to start an uproar in Santa Ana."

"That points to Barrio," said JD. "The more you know, the less you know, and you know why? Because the more you know, the more questions you can ask."

JD knew he had a story in his head that had formed watching the rain, but it was too literary, too much like a novel to be the truth.

"Who was the last person to see the judicial cop alive? I saw him yesterday in the park at five o'clock in the afternoon. After that . . ."

A hypothesis occurred to him, even more like a novel, without any foundation. A hypothesis that implied there had been a traitor in Santa Ana. That happens in novels, doesn't it? And he had even another hunch, but the story of the Chinese widow belonged to another novel. He had to move, science wouldn't provide the answers he was looking for.

"Greñas and Russian, your turn to investigate the movements of the judicial cop since yesterday. Barrientos, could you get Blackie's helper from the hotel and bring him here?"

"We don't have jurisdiction there. I'd have to go in unarmed."

"Can you?"

"I'll bring him."

"Popochas, get the motorcycle ready, we're going to see the gringos."

Like a small army, the members of the Santa Ana police force began to clean their pistols, smooth their moustaches, comb their hair, shake off fatigue. Better to get moving than to study science.

"And me?" asked Merenciano.

"It's your turn to erase the chalkboard."

52.

Tattoos

A North American outside his country is a vulnerable creature who has to surround himself with bottled soft drinks, toothpaste, and electric can-openers if he doesn't want to die of loneliness.

José Daniel tried to confirm that idea, which he had used in various novels, on entering the neighborhood of San Carlos and seeing the small duplex houses with ten square yards of garden in front and a hose ensuring the brilliant green of the grass although it had rained that morning.

"Lómax, what will you be when you grow up?"

"A cop, chief."

"Don't you think that's a very routine job?"

"But a hell of a lot happens . . . Which house are we going to?"

"The first one you like."

Lómax was slowly braking the motorcycle, coming to rest

ten yards from a one-armed gringo who was sweeping the
yard with his one hand.

José Daniel got off the bike.

"Pispanish?" he asked directly.

"Yes, I speak a little," replied the gringo, smiling at him.

"José Daniel Fierro, chief of police of Santa Ana," said
JD, offering his hand.

"I've read your book," said the North American, pressing
firmly. "Johnnie Walker."

"That's a real name?" asked JD, disconcerted, slipping
into English.

"No, just a nickname." He turned to the inside of the
house. "Betty, the chief of police. The writer!"

Betty stepped out, wearing an enormous apron, giving
every indication she had been making an apple pie.

"I've read *Notebook*."

"Did you like it?"

"Very fine plot and the general idea. I also read *All Night
Shooting and Dancing*, that's the one Betty likes most.
Right?"

"Yes. It's my favorite. JW is also a writer."

"And what do you write?" asked JD, letting himself fall
onto the lush lawn. JW followed suit.

"History, mostly."

José Daniel took out the photograph.

"Do you know her?"

"Anne—they killed her in town the other day, right?"
said Betty, demonstrating fluent Spanish.

"What do you know about her?"

"The one who could tell you more about her is Jerry
Martínez, they're very good friends. Let's go," said JW,
getting up.

Lómax and Chief Fierro followed the North American couple, crossed the garden next door, and climbed a porch.

"Do you have books in English, chief?" whispered Lómax.

"Four novels."

"Jerry, the chief of police of Santa Ana," Betty said to a big Chicano who came out to meet them on the porch. He had a moustache as good as that of the chief of police.

"Did you know Anne Goldin?"

"Of course," said the Chicano. "We were very good friends. She was a good person."

"Did you see her Monday?"

"She came by here in the morning to bring me a book that my sister sent me from San Jose . . ."

"What was Anne doing in Santa Ana?"

Jerry stared at the chief of police, then decided to answer. "She came to see the father of Tommy, her son, a guy she located here after looking for many years. A strange story, she never said much about it . . . She came to take our photos, and when we talked we found we had a lot in common, she had studied in San Jose with my sister. And we saw each other a few times last year, and now she brought me that book. Last year she said she'd be back because she had found Tommy's father here in Santa Ana."

"Didn't she tell you who he was?"

"No. Nor did I ask. I don't go out much. I can't move around much because of the lesion." He lifted his shirt and showed an enormous scar above his liver.

"Nothing? Not one clue?"

"That was last year, this year we didn't even talk about it. She said she had brought a photo of Tommy to show me but that she'd left it at the hotel. And last year nothing. Just that. That Tommy's father lived in Santa Ana and that she had found him."

JD shook hands again, declined an invitation to coffee and cake, promised to return when things calmed down to talk about literature and to read JW's manuscript, and went to the motorcycle with Lómax.

"Chief!" cried Jerry after them. "She said something about uniting the tattoos . . . I didn't understand very well, but she had a tattoo on her arm, right?"

53.

Declarations

―――――――――――――――――――――――

"That guy is absolutely mad. He's having romantic problems so he plays Zitarrosa's song "Stephanie" fifty times. I've gotten twenty protest calls," said Fritz to JD, who had once again become the arbiter of minor conflicts at Radio Santa Ana.

"I have a gift for you in the office," said Barrientos when he saw JD in the hallway.

"Who knows where the judicial was all night yesterday," reported Greñas.

"The mine is threatening to declare a lockout," Mercado informed him when he passed by the door to the bathroom.

"Barrientos, call Dr. Jiménez, ask him if the judicial had a tattoo—they must have him on the table by now and can look him over," said José Daniel, passing through the door to his office.

"It wasn't me, chief," said Blackie's assistant, tied up in the chair of the chief of police.

"Me either," replied José Daniel to gain time.

54.

Dear Ana/April 22

~~~~~~

Dear Ana/April 22

The novel continues. It is a novel about tattoos. Its characters are a commander of the judicial police who has a tattoo on his ass that says: *Who arrives here does not leave alive*; also a North American who has a tiny rose on her forearm with the phrase *Loneliness is the heart of life*. Also, so it won't be too easy, an albino gunman who has a plumed serpent tattooed on his left arm.

As you will see, the novel appears to belong to Vázquez Montalbán and not to me.

The protagonist is a Chinese who dedicates himself to commerce and has a double life, because in the back room of one of his businesses he also practices the forbidden art of the exotic Japanese tattoo (it's a problem that he's Chinese and the tattoos are Japanese, but it can be resolved).

I have various problems: one of them is that the child in the photo has no Asiatic features at all, the other is that I don't feel like going to see the tattoos of the Priísta cacique.

The novel, nevertheless, despite my indecisiveness, goes on filling up with weird stiffs and out-of-place confessions.

What do you think? Tomorrow I'll send you Chapter Three. An enormous kiss in the solitude of this monkish cell.

JD

55.

Resign? No way!

~~~~~~

"I came to see you because . . ."

"Cut it out, would you?" said JD, leaning back on his
metal cot. "All I need now is for someone to arrive at
the hotel and say, 'I came to Comala because they told
me . . . ' "

Benjamín sat on the carpet at the foot of the bed. "Blind
Man told me what the gunman told him. The shots fired at
you the other day did not come from on high. I don't know
if this is better or worse, bu. if you want to resign, that seems
reasonable to me."

"Resign? No way!" said JD euphorically. Benjamín had
interrupted a seriously drunken interlude. And JD was only
halfway to his intended alcoholic destination.

"Moreover, things are heating up heavy, my chief."

"Did you bring a bottle? I can't give you any of mine.
And least of all unless you stop moving, asshole," said JD.

"Son of a whore, you're shitfaced drunk and I didn't even

notice. I'll be right back," said the mayor of Santa Ana, and went out, leaving the door open.

JD did not bother to close it. He lowered his trousers and showed his balls to a maid who went running away down the hall.

Benjamín returned in five minutes with his own bottle of brandy, closed the door, sat on the floor and drank a quarter of it in one gulp.

"To catch up with you, bastard."

"You're going to get very fucked up, Señor Mayor, and then the fucking Chinese will get hold of you and cover you with tattoos on all sides, very weird all covered with tattoos, on the sixteenth of September you're going to look like hell ringing the independence bell all covered with tattoos."

"That's what I wanted to talk about. We won't make it to the sixteenth, Señor Chief of Police. They're going to fuck us up first."

"The Chinese?"

"The Chinese will peel our dicks. Lick our balls."

"Our balls," said JD, pointing at his with difficulty. "Our eggs."

"No, I'm talking about the government."

"The government won't lick my balls."

"The governor passed a petition to the state congress dissolving the government of Santa Ana. The state press is accusing me of the murders. They say that you want to trap Barrio and that we're going to use that pretext to kill him. Judicials from all over the state are arriving and closing in on the land invaders. They're bringing the whole works."

"They must want to give us a fucking tattoo on the ass."

"What the fuck is this with the tattoos?"

"No. Let's change the subject. Fuck."

To join the mood, Benjamín dispatched another quarter of the bottle in one gulp that to JD appeared interminable. He took one a bit shorter. Good brandy and bad were meant to be savored.

"What was I saying?" asked Benjamín.

"Now you're drunk, Benjamín."

"I'm never drunk."

"Me either," said JD, and he got up to vomit in the washbasin.

"What a miserable drunk! Police drunk."

"I am a democratic cop," said José Daniel, trying to keep the spittle from running down his lips. Stumbling, he reached the bed and fell down again. The bottle was still there at his right. He took another drink to rinse his mouth.

"You mean shit to me, Benjamín. Santa Ana means shit to me. I was an asshole writing a novel in Mexico City and Santa Ana means shit to me."

"I told you. You mean shit to me, too . . . Who killed them?"

"Who the fuck knows. Do you think I'd be here getting plastered if I knew?" said José Daniel with difficulty.

"They're going to fuck us over."

"No way. I'll find the killers tomorrow, the fag bastards."

"You think so?"

"Of course, the fucking murderers are whores, I'll fuck them tomorrow."

"You mean shit to me, Chief Fierro," said Benjamín before vomiting in the washbasin.

"Son of a bitch, you're fucking wasted," said José Daniel Fierro, smiling at his bottle, which moved less than the mayor.

56.

You're the Only Ones

~~~~~~~~~~~~~~~~~~~~~~~~~~~~~~~~~~~~~~

It dawned rainy again and the city was covered with damp three-color posters announcing a PRI demonstration at six o'clock. From the door of the Hotel Florida, José Daniel Fierro, tasting metal from his hangover, looked at them wondering if he should cross the street in the middle of the downpour.

The patrol car, with its splendid red and black paint job, stopped before the door to the hotel.

"They fired on the campesinos last night," said Blind Man, opening the door. "Benjamín is giving a press conference right now, do you want to go?"

"Let's go and visit the Calle Escondida."

"Alone?"

"Just us and our shadows."

"Do you want to read the press of the state capital, *El Heraldo* and *El Independiente*?"

"What does it say?"

"They're arguing in the local congress if they should invade us. Now there's a PRI demonstration and also a meeting of the Popular Organization."

"Does the PRI have people in Santa Ana?"

"A few, the rest they bring in from other places."

"Let's go."

Blind Man started up the car and reached the highway in five minutes through the empty streets.

Calle Escondida was full of automobiles. The grim-faced drivers, some of them armed with automatic rifles that they held ready despite the rain, began to move toward the patrol car.

"Say the word," whispered Blind Man.

"What time is the demonstration?"

"At six, they start at six."

"We'll come back then."

The patrol car started up in reverse. A pair of shots rang out, the windshield shattered by a bullet. Blind Man braked and took out his .45.

"Hold it, Blind Man, we'll be back," said JD, grabbing his arm.

Santa Ana was inundated by music. Every two minutes the alternating voices of Fritz and Canales announced the demonstration.

Benjamín was waiting for them in the office.

"The mission of the police force of Santa Ana is to prevent the two demonstrations from meeting. Let's establish a blockade on Calle Revolución, in these three blocks. We can't have any provocations. The national press is in Santa Ana, that can serve as pressure. Can you do it?"

"At Barrio's house there are some fifty gunmen, with automatic arms, against six of us," said Blind Man.

"We'll see what he can do," said José Daniel.

"How do you feel?" asked Benjamín.

"Like an asshole," replied José Daniel Fierro.

"That makes two of us," replied the mayor.

"You're the only ones," said the assistant chief of police of Santa Ana.

57.

Dear Ana/April 23

‑‑

Dear Ana/April 23

The novel continues:

It is a novel of games. People die, and the ones who kill them think they're killing for a motive, but they do it at the suggestion of others, who in turn have another motive, and so on. So that no one really knows exactly why people die in the book.

The characters are an American who comes to Mexico to see her ex-husband to get child support from him, the ex-husband who refuses to give it to her, a pair of hired killers who kill her to pressure her ex-husband, the enemy of the ex-husband who really directs them against him, an associate of the ex-husband who negotiates with the killers, and the town's disoriented sheriff who veers between synthetic glory and madness.

The beauty of the novel is that the sheriff discovers nothing, only that things simply happen. That's what I like about this novel—that it has no ending, no closing, but is, as I've said of my days in Santa Ana, like life itself.

What do you think?

I miss you. JD

58.

Notes for the History of the Radical City Government of
Santa Ana
José Daniel Fierro

~~~~~~

In these last two years, what did the radical city government
contribute to the inhabitants of the town?

The question is not easy. It is a government that has not
had even a month of normalcy. It has never been able to
receive the entire funding it is entitled to. Even so, we can
gather some ideas among those that the whole world speaks
of, those outside and those inside:

An honest administration of funds, that had many repercus-
sions in minor details: city cleaning, the reconstruction of the
market, the birth of six production cooperatives and two big
ones of consumers, a big hydraulic irrigation works, a cultural
project that I have never been able to see but that everyone
talks about behind the municipal House of Culture, the new
popular secondary school, a healthier relationship with the
authorities, a moralization of the police force, efficient control

of business, the reconstruction of the three colonial monuments that are in the city. Things like that.

It is hard to judge based on these things. You would have to have lived in Santa Ana three years ago and I did not.

Maybe most important is that the people were mobilized. Or the inverse, the government was mobilized by the people. And this I have seen. These phenomena of mobilization of the immobilizable, the advance by centuries in a few days, the transformed mentality, are difficult to see in a country in which complaint substitutes for action.

59.

Streets

━━━━━━━━━━━━━━━━━━━━━━━━━━━━━━━━━━

"The patrol car in the middle of the street. On the block that follows the metal barriers. Greñas with the bike at the corner of Revolución and Lerdo. Barrientos in the center. Russian and Merenciano at Revolución and Seis. The street cleared of cars, so that we can see with a simple glance. Blockades down the middle."

At his back the miners go by, formed in columns of four, with axes and picks, with clubs. The noise of the crowd grows in the streets beaten by the drizzle, that fine rain that does not dampen but goes on entering the clothing until it reaches the body. Radio Santa Ana is silent. This morning, the broadcasting plant was sabotaged, the technicians are trying to repair it. They succeed in the middle of the demonstration, and suddenly Benjamín's speech fills the empty streets of Santa Ana and the packed plaza. His voice full of fury: *Let them go, they have nothing to do with our city. No one can negotiate with our liberty. No one can come and tell us how we should live, how we should organize our days, our passions, our needs. No one can come here to deny us the right to work honestly, the right to work together, the right to not let ourselves be exploited. The right to be the free town of Santa Ana. No congress of paid deputies who kowtow to the central power can decree that we do not exist. Here we are! We are the people of Santa Ana! And there will be no voices, nor votes, nor newspapers, nor tanks that can deny this simple but definitive truth: We exist. We do exist. We do exist. Santa Ana will win!* and the rhythm of *Santa Ana will win Santa Ana will win* was repeated like thunder and threatened to tumble the walls and electric cables and to stop the rain.

José Daniel feels the clamor striking him in the back while he tries to guess if the provocation is advancing through the drizzle. If the black city will spit out death. It gets dark. There are only shadows.

"I don't think they're coming," says Barrientos. "They must not have gotten very many people together."

Night falls. The first groups begin to return from the demonstration of the PO. José Daniel orders the patrol retired.

60.

Nocturne

~~~~~~

"**M**y neighbor stands up at night when he thinks that nobody sees him," said the voice on the phone. José Daniel does not need to ask who was its owner. He reacted as a character out of Earl Derr Biggers.

"What else can you tell me, Mrs. Ling?"

"Since yesterday the house of my other neighbor is full of armed gentlemen."

"I thank you very much for the information . . ."

"The American girl saw both of them the afternoon they killed her. She was first in one house and then in the other."

José Daniel scratched his head.

"I thank you, madam."

"I'll be watching them, I'll let you know."

"Very kind of you," said the chief of police of Santa Ana as he hung up.

José Daniel had been bathing when the call came through, but now he could not find the strength to get back under the shower. He was cold. On his table, together with the manuscript he had started about the history of the radical city government of Santa Ana, were Anne's photos. There were two he wanted to see: those of the engineer López, the false cripple, and that of Melchor Barrio, the PRI cacique of Santa Ana. There must be some clue in those photos. *She visited them both.* He already knew that, the photos had already told him. Hours later they killed her. What took place during those visits? Who ordered her killed? Why naked and in the church? What could the gunman and the judicial have told her? What the fuck was happening in this city that was beginning to catch fire? José Daniel had no answers. It was not a logical problem. What did his nephew Javier say when he had no information? *Not computable.* Just so, not computable. He had not even been able to sit down in front of the two men. The false paralytic, the cacique. Was it really useful to know the truth? Would the truth stop the whirlwind from being unleashed on Santa Ana?

José Daniel got dressed again. The rain beat on the window.

At the door of the Hotel Florida, Blind Man waited for him in the Volkswagen patrol car, smoking a cigarette.

"I thought we would have nocturnal visitors, chief."

"You second-guess me too much, Blind Man, I'm going to put you on the list of suspects."

"Of the judicial and Blackie, what the hell, but the gringa no, please."

The automobile took the same route toward the outskirts of Santa Ana but did not enter the neighborhood.

"The paralytic is not paralytic," said JD.

"How do you know?"

"You see, I too have my resources."

"Are we going straight? Do we go sideways? Do we hide? Do we show ourselves? Do we go to the engineer's house? Are we going to Barrio's house? Are we just out for fresh air? You tell me."

"Rule number seventeen of the detective novels I don't like: the murderer is the one we least suspect."

"And rule seventeen of the novels you do like?"

"The murderer is a son of a bitch who almost escapes."

"Which do you prefer?"

"A combination: the paralytic who is not paralytic and Barrio. Together."

"Let's check them out."

The car turned in again at the entrance to the neighborhood. Three times they had been to this street: La Escondida. Barrio's house was dark. There were lights at the house of the engineer, and a dim light on the second floor of the Chinese widow's house.

"Barrio is out of town. He must be in the capital, negotiating the booty, chief."

"Let's go to the engineer."

He knew the man who opened the door, he appeared in the photos pushing the wheelchair. He was bigger in real life than in the photos.

"We would like to speak with Engineer López," said Blind Man.

López appeared, pushing his wheelchair through a swinging door that apparently led to the kitchen. José Daniel took off his cap and hung it coquettishly on the barrel of his gun. Blind Man remained standing near by, measuring the majordomo.

"Who are you?"

"Pal, that's what I should be asking you," said the paralytic who wasn't. "But I've seen declarations of yours in the press with photos, and I even saw you on a television show years ago."

"You are not paralyzed. You are hiding out in Santa Ana. You are Anne's ex-husband and the father of her child. You have a name that is not López. The red car was put in front of your house to pressure you. But you did not kill her."

José Daniel grew still. He waited. Then he walked toward the man and took off his dark glasses.

The man had gray eyes. José Daniel heard a noise at his

back and guessed that Blind Man had taken charge of the majordomo. He didn't even turn around.

"Let me see your arm," said JD.

The man remained immobile, looking nowhere, seated in his chair. JD took his left arm and rolled up his sleeve. Nothing. He repeated the operation with his right arm. There was the small tattoo, a rose, with the same words, but in Spanish: *La soledad es el corazón de la vida.*

"I can take your photo without dark glasses and circulate it among the journalists at City Hall. Surely someone there will recognize you. It's only a matter of time."

The man did not try to meet his eyes. Immutable, every hair in place, a gray cravat at his neck. A portrait of other times. JD turned around. Blind Man was tying up the majordomo with a venetian blind cord.

"Blind Man, bring the fucking Polaroid from the car, it's in the glove box."

Barrientos finished his work, checked the knots, and left the house. JD turned back to the man in the wheelchair, who was looking with curiosity at his own tattoo, as if seeing it for the first time. Lew Archer would now begin to speak with the character, carrying him back in time. That was what fascinated Ross Macdonald, men who could not return to the past. José Daniel did not give a damn. He only wanted the truth. Blind Man came in with the camera. José Daniel Fierro took four or five photos of the man in the wheelchair. He gave them to Blind Man, who left the house in silence.

"We could save ourselves some trouble," said the chief of police. The man did not respond, only gave him a sad smile. José Daniel fell into an armchair with his shotgun between his hands. It was a temporary home, someone had chosen the furniture for the silent man, someone had decided that the brocades went well with a mustard-colored carpet, someone had brought the bar and even filled it with exotic bottles.

"You have a name," said JD to say something.

"There's a suitcase with half a million dollars in the hall closet. Let me buy your shotgun."

"What do you want it for?"

The man shut up again, looking at his tattoo. Then he got up. JD raised his shotgun, but there was no aggression in the movement. The man went to the closet and returned with the suitcase, he put it between them. He pushed away the wheelchair as if he would never need it again, and opened the suitcase on the middle of the rug. It was full of hundred-dollar bills. Five thousand one hundred dollar bills, calculated JD, fifty prettily wrapped packets of one hundred.

"I don't need the shotgun, I have a pistol. I only want two minutes . . ."

"Your neighbor is not here, the lights are out, those two minutes won't help you at all . . . Let's make another exchange. I'll trade you the photos of your son and the photos of Anne's body in the church for another story." JD looked in his shirt pocket. There were the Polaroids of the dead girl in the church. He passed them to him. The man took them as if they would burn him. He looked at them one by one.

"If you don't tell me the story, I'll guess it."

"I don't give a shit," said the man without taking his eyes from one of the photographs.

Shock therapy, JD told himself, and went on pressuring while he stroked the trigger.

"What did Barrio offer you? Security forever? For that he ordered her killed, to go on giving you orders, and in passing, to stir things up a bit here in town. He's a man with a practical mind, a shame I've never met him."

The man let the photos fall in the suitcase.

"I never saw the photos of the child."

"I have them at the office. I'll show you when we get there."

"You don't want the money?"

"I guess not."

"The shotgun was for me. Barrio is at home, dead. He's

naked in a bathtub. With a shot through each eye. I turned out the lights when I left."

José Daniel smiled at him.

"You don't want the money?"

"No, I don't need it. Santa Ana pays me seventy-two thousand pesos twice a month and I get something in royalties." He considered explaining that Goldman Verlag was about to publish three of his novels and that they paid in marks, but it wasn't worth his while.

The man arranged the bills and closed the suitcase again. He took the photos carefully and gave them to the chief of police, who returned them to the pocket of his khaki shirt.

"What a bunch of shit, eh?" said the chief of police of Santa Ana, for something to say . . . This ending was no good, he felt trapped in someone else's story.

The patrol car braked before the door of the mansion; the efficient Barrientos would carry out the rest of the drama. But the story did not belong to him. Perhaps a little?

61.

Dear Ana/April 23 (II)

Dear Ana/April 23

End of the novel: The town sheriff understands nothing, although he learns everything without meaning to. The bad guys of the story kill each other off, and he stays behind watching the graveyard.

It was a novel of "uncovered passions," but not of "hidden passions" because nobody writes about them anymore.

Everything turns around a town cacique without a tattoo, who has a lot of dirt on those who do have tattoos. He gives orders to one while he hides him, orders another to kill her, orders others to put the red car in a certain street. It's a bit complicated, the novel. I don't know if I want to write it, I don't think so, it lacks a hook, dramatic architecture, the negative characters (as my Cuban friends would say) are badly drawn. I don't think I'd like to write it.

Rather I'm sure I would not like to write it.

But I love you. JD

62.

Here at Radio Santa Ana

~~~~~~

"What's happening, chief?" asked Canales at the door to City Hall.

The plaza was full of campfires, the people were waiting for something. José Daniel entered, accompanied by Blind Man, who brought in the former chief of acquisitions of Pemex, who had disappeared two years ago with eleven million dollars in a suitcase, bound by toy handcuffs that rattled from every link in the chain.

"What's happening here?"

"The state congress dissolved the government of Santa Ana a few hours ago. The cabinet is meeting . . . And what have we here?"

"A pathetic jerk. He just killed Barrio."

"Piss up a rope! Now the shit's hit the fan!"

"One down," said Blind Man, slapping the properly

dressed man on the back, who despite everything had not a hair out of place or a wrinkle in his gray cravat.

"Take him to the office, Blind Man. I'm going to see Benjamín. Call the journalists. I'm going to get Barrio's death off the back of the town."

At that moment, loudspeakers began to sound across the town. Surprisingly, not with the "Venceremos" but with "Penélope" by Serrat.

"Fucking Fritz, he's completely flipped out," said Juan Carlos.

The cabinet room was full of smoke. Little blue clouds that ascended from the big table. The lawyer Mercado was by the phone.

"They already gave out the news in Mexico City. Before they finished voting they had already had a press conference, the representative of the local government there. What fucking mugs they are!"

"Okay, we already know what we have to do," said Benjamín. His eyes were irritated. "Macario, tell the boys at Radio Santa Ana that the government is invoking a total and indefinite general strike, close the markets, close the highways. Pass the declarations on to the press. Half the government stays here, the other half, along with the leadership of the PO, already knows where they have to go. Scabs to be dealt with by the neighborhood groups. Serafín, get moving. You have to advise all the communities from here to La Cañada. Every one of them."

The people began to get to their feet. Benjamín came toward José Daniel.

"Shit, we wouldn't have brought you to town for so little time."

"I got my month's pay, and the month isn't over."

"I think I should meet with all the police and speak with them a bit, but I don't feel like it. Blind Man Barrientos knows the emergency plan, and knows about guarding the arms. All in good time . . . I think you should resign and get together with the press. These next few days are going to be a bit brutal, and it wouldn't be a bad idea for Santa Ana to have its own chronicler.''

"Let somebody else tell the story,'' said José Daniel, slapping the mayor on the back.

"Aren't you going to talk to the people outside the building, Benjamín?'' asked the young leader of the miners of shaft number three. José Daniel had seen him on other occasions.

"Right now,'' said Benjamín Correa, stretching.

"I solved the mystery.''

Correa looked at him with surprise.

"You solved it?''

"It solved itself. I'll tell you. You know, Barrio was killed.''

"By one of us?''

"No, one of them.''

"What do you know, that's good news,'' said Benjamín, going out on the balcony.

José Daniel climbed down the stairs, past the mural of hell. He stared at the image of the Priísta cacique whom he had never met, and imagined him in a bathtub with two shots in his head.

At the entrance to the studios of Radio Santa Ana, Canales stopped him. Fritz was broadcasting: "People of Santa Ana, we have to inform you that a couple of minutes ago two army tanks entered by the main highway.''

In that moment, all the loudspeakers began to sound. Fritz had put on a record of the National Anthem.

Wearily, José Daniel covered the steps that led to his office.

63.

Dear Ana/April 27

~~~~~~

Dear Ana/April 27
   I got Canales and Fritz as cellmates, together with my
assistant chief, Barrientos. We are designing a four-dimen-
sional chess game. Canales organized a workshop on the
poetry of Nezahualcóyotl. I'm writing a novel. Although it
causes me remorse to say so, in the midst of so much injustice,
of so much aggression hurled at Santa Ana, I am a happy
man. Tell the spectators in Mexico City and New York, and
in Madrid, that I'm a happy man. I suppose you'll wait to
divorce me until they let us out. Meanwhile, you could just
as well send me the aspirin and the blue turtleneck sweater
that I've asked you for.

                                                I love you, JD
P.S. I've kept my baseball cap.

"Why in the circus?"